MULTICULTURAL FABLES AND FAIRY TALES

STORIES AND ACTIVITIES TO PROMOTE LITERACY AND CULTURAL AWARENESS

◆

by Tara McCarthy

SCHOLASTIC
PROFESSIONAL BOOKS

NEW YORK ◆ TORONTO ◆ LONDON ◆ AUCKLAND ◆ SYDNEY

ACKNOWLEDGMENTS

Special thanks to Marian Reiner and Bill Gordh
for their help with this project.

"Coyote Places the Stars" from *Giving Birth to Thunder, Sleeping With His Daughter* by Barry Lopez.
Copyright © 1977 by Barry Holstun Lopez. Reprinted by permission of Andrews & McMeel.
All rights reserved.

"The Five Water-Spirits" from *Thirty Indians Legends of Canada* by Margaret Bemister, published by
Douglas and McIntyre. Copyright © 1973 by Margaret Bemister. Reprinted with permission.

"Hare Tricks Lion" originally titled "Numskull and the Rabbit" from *Many Lands, Many Stories* retold by
David Conger. Copyright © 1987 by Charles E. Tuttle Co., Inc. Adapted and reprinted by permission of
Charles E. Tuttle Co., Inc.

"How Butterflies Came to Be" from *Keepers of the Animals: Native American Animal Stories and Wildlife
Activities for Children* by Michael J. Caduto and Joseph Bruchac, Fulcrum Publishing, Inc., 350 Indiana Street,
#350, Golden, Colorado 80401 (303) 277-1623. Copyright © 1991 by Michael J. Caduto and Joseph
Bruchac. Adapted and reprinted by permission of the publisher.

"How the Finch Got Her Colors" from *Stories that Never Grow Old* edited by Watty Piper. Copyright
© 1938, renewed 1966 by Platt & Munk, Publishers. Adapted and reprinted by permission of Platt & Munk,
Publishers.

"Mei-Ling and the Dragon" originally titled "The Dragon's Tears" from *Japanese Children's Stories* edited by
Florence Sakade. Copyright © 1959 by Charles E. Tuttle Co., Inc. Adapted and reprinted by permission of
Charles E. Tuttle Co., Inc.

"The Singing Monster" originally titled "The Monster That Never Was" adapted from *Agikuyu Folk Tales* by
Ngumbu Njururi. Copyright © 1966 by Oxford University Press. Extensive research failed to locate author
and/or copyright holder of this work.

"Tortoise Tricks Leopard" originally titled "Land Turtle and Leopard" adapted from *African Folklore* by
Richard M. Dorson. Copyright © 1972 by Richard M. Dorson. Extensive research failed to located the
author and/or copyright holder of this work.

Designed by Sue Boria, Design Five

Cover design by Vincent Ceci

Cover illustration by Donna Perrone

Interior illustration by Joanna Roy

ISBN 0-590-49231-4

TABLE OF CONTENTS

USING FOLK LITERATURE IN YOUR CLASSROOM

Folktales are stories that have been handed down through the centuries orally. People of all cultures still tell these age-old stories aloud. Once they are written down, they become folk literature. This book recounts 24 of these stories, accompanied by teaching suggestions and activity sheets… enough to launch your students into an exciting, participatory study of traditional tales and the cultures from which they come.

Folk literature is well-suited to elementary classrooms. Here's why:

◆ Folktales are fun. They are full of humor, adventure, and suspense.

◆ Folktales provide a storehouse of metaphors, symbols, and repeated phrases that children can easily assimilate into their own language.

◆ Folktales help children to clarify their own values and concerns about appropriate behavior, and to develop concepts about the meanings of big ideas such as truth, courage, and kindness. Further, as Bruno Bettelheim has pointed out in *The Uses of Enchantment: The Meaning and Importance of Fairy Tales* (Alfred A. Knopf, 1976), the physical confrontations between the protagonist and her or his scary antagonist allow children to "stare down," accept, and resolve their very real and unconscious conflicts and fears about the world. Externalized and represented as folktale "villains," these fears can be acknowledged, referred to, and discussed in the safe context of a shared story.

◆ Folktales can enhance reading comprehension and critical thinking. As children compare, contrast, and evaluate the tales, they develop their abilities not only to enjoy literature but to articulate why they enjoy it as well.

◆ Folktales expose children to literature that can boost writing skills. The tales have stock characters, predictable patterns, and reiterated themes, making them accessible models for student writing.

◆ Folktales serve as natural springboards into other areas of the curriculum, thus helping to build and enrich an integrated curriculum.

◆ Folk literature can build literacy. References to "sour grapes,"remarks about "frogs turning into princes," and metaphors like "sly as a fox" originate in folktales and in other facets of the oral tradition and have become part of our general culture. Exposure to traditional stories helps children understand and appreciate these references when they come across them in everyday life.

BUILDING APPRECIATION OF CULTURAL DIVERSITY

By reading and discussing folktales from around the world, children develop insights into different cultures and their values. For example, when reading "How Flying Fish Came to Be," young readers discover the respect the people of New Guinea have for natural resources. In reading the Ghanaian tale "Why Chickens and Hawks Are Enemies," students sense the value placed by that culture on keeping promises. Tales about the trickster Coyote illustrate for children the Native-American emphasis on combining cleverness with creativity.

Still, as diverse as folktales may be in their cultural settings, they usually emphasize some value or sense of reality common to all cultures and recognizable to almost all children. For example, the value of honesty is stressed in folktales from places as culturally different as Japan, Greece, and Germany. Traditional storytellers of many lands, including Kenya and China, emphasize the importance of courage and common sense. Awe and respect for nature shows up in tales from Native Americans of Canada and the Southwest, as well as in stories from Belgium and Brazil. By enjoying folktales together, your students will not only come to appreciate their own ethnic traditions, but will also find that they have much in common with all people.

BUILDING CULTURAL CONNECTIONS ACROSS THE CURICULUM

You can use the folktales in this book to reinforce or initiate skills and cultural understandings in different curricular areas. Here are some general examples of strategies and projects. (The introductory page for each tale suggests more specific applications.)

◆ **GEOGRAPHY:** When introducing each story, use a globe or a world map to show the country from which each story comes. If your students are already studying that area, discuss features such as bodies of water, climate, and natural resources of that region. Ask students to reread or listen again to the story to find hints of these settings.

◆ **SOCIAL STUDIES:** (1) Invite students to study illustrations to find out how people in the culture used to live, dress, and eat, then discuss how this culture has changed and how it has remained the same. For example, after enjoying the fairy tale "The Frog Prince," a group of students can research and report on what medieval castles were like and then compare them with modern homes. (2) Encourage students who have recently come from other lands to tell about their customs and holidays. For example, after the class enjoys the fairy tale "Mei-Ling and the Dragon," a student might report on how the dragon is used as a good-luck symbol in celebrating the Chinese New Year. (3) Invite students to share stories and sayings from the cultures their families represent.

◆ **SCIENCE:** (1) Animals are featured in many folktales. Students can do research to find facts about indigenous animals in the part of the world from which a tale comes, then make charts comparing and contrasting the fictional and actual appearance and behavior of these animals. (2) From time to time, discuss technological changes, such as transportation. For example, the princess and her new husband in "The Frog Prince" ride in a horse-drawn coach, and Mei-Ling in "Mei-Ling and the Dragon" travels in a sailing ship. What kinds of transportation might these characters use in today's world? How have changes in technology affected the lives of people in specific countries and cultural groups, including those of the ones represented by your students?

◆ **THE ARTS:** Introduce your students to the music and visual arts of the cultural groups or historical periods represented in the stories.
(1) Reproductions of paintings and crafts from different cultures are available in many art books. Make copies to display in the classroom while students are

reading and exploring a story. Discuss the forms and techniques, and encourage students to try them out in the illustrations they make for their own stories. Some students may be able to bring to class reproductions or authentic examples of the objects, such as pottery or wall hangings. (2) You may wish to play taped music from the represented culture as the class reads or listens to a story. (See the Bibliography, page 108, for sources.) Invite students to identify the kinds of instruments used (such as strings, wind instruments, or voice), to duplicate the rhythms with classroom band instruments, to make up words to go with the music, or to act out the story with the music as a background.

HOW THE FOLK LITERATURE IN THIS BOOK IS ORGANIZED

Scholars generally sort folktales into groups, such as fables, trickster stories, pourquoi ("why") stories, and legends. However, the groups often overlap. For example, many fables involve tricksters; many pourquoi stories straddle the fine line between an imaginary, fun story about the origin of some natural characteristic (as in "How the Beetle Got Her Colors") and a sacred, serious story (as in "The Five Water-Spirits"). Similarly, fables are generally presumed to have only animal characters; yet there are humans in many fables, such as "The Milkmaid and Her Pail."

This overlapping acknowledged, the stories in this book are divided into four sections: *Trickster Tales*, *Fables*, *"Why" Stories*, and *Fairy Tales*. The characteristics of the different types of tales are detailed in the Teaching Suggestion pages that open each section. As students study the different types of tales, encourage them to identify and discuss how they overlap.

GENERAL TEACHING TIPS

1. Use the introductory page before each section and the teaching tips before each story to familiarize yourself with the type of tale and with suggested procedures and activities.

2. Whenever possible, tell a story aloud instead of reading it directly from the book. To do this, you will need to pre-read the tale and become so familiar with it that you can add your own details and style. In telling the story rather than reading it, you will be an inheritor and transmitter of the oral tradition in which folktales are imbedded. Your tell-aloud strategy will encourage your students to tell stories aloud, too, in a dramatic and personal way.

3. Distribute copies of the stories to students or pairs of students. Invite students to read them aloud to each other, adding their own details and illustrations. Students can also include these copies in their Folktale Portfolios. (See page 10.)

4. Use the activity sheets to help students reinforce and apply reading skills and to motivate them to give their personal responses to folktales. Students can carry out the activities individually or with reading and writing partners. They can make the completed sheets and related projects, such as puppets and collages, part of their Folktale Portfolios.

5. Be prepared to answer students' questions about why the protagonists in so many folktales are male. There is a male orientation in most folk literature: That is the way the stories have been traditionally told. This book strives to be authentic in the retellings so it does not "correct" gender-bias. If you wish to discuss this male orientation with your students, you can link it to your social studies curriculum: What did boys and men usually do in "the old days"? What did girls and women usually do in those times? How do traditional tales reflect these gender-specific roles? How have roles changed in modern times?As your students model their own stories on folktales, encourage them to use female protagonists as tricksters, as fable or "why" story characters, and as the courageous rescuer or problem-solver in fairy tales.

6. Provide follow-up folk literature for students to read and discuss. Refer to the Bibliography on page 108 for suggested titles. Invite students to share the books with the class by giving oral book reports, discussing the cultures from which the stories came, identifying the tale-type, and acting out the stories with classmates.

CLASS PROJECTS, COOPERATIVE LEARNING

1. Whole-Class: A whole-class project is suggested for each of the four types of tales. These projects result in visual organizers for display. For example, the visual organizer for *Trickster Tales* is a series of Story Clock Organizers that help students track sequence in different trickster stories; the visual organizer for *Fairy Tales* is a Fairy Tale Chart Organizer that leads students to classify the common components of fairy tales. These visual organizers help students discuss the tales and get ideas and prompts for the stories they will write.

2. Cooperative Learning and Partners: You will also find suggestions for helping students to work together to enhance and share their enjoyment of folk literature.

For example, as students enjoy "why" stories, groups can make picture panels showing the major incidents in a tale. Or, as students read fables, one partner can state a problem for the advice column of an imaginary newspaper, then his or her partner can present a solution.

STUDENTS AS WRITERS: PORTFOLIOS AND STORIES

Through reading and discussing folk literature, students discover manageable patterns on which to build their own stories. They also come to realize that within these patterns there is latitude for the writer's original ideas.

PORTFOLIOS AS A DISCOVERY PROCESS

To help students reinforce and personalize what they are learning about folktale-types, encourage them to keep individual portfolios for each type as they read the stories.

The portfolios can include:

◆ copies of the folktales;

◆ activity sheets and their outcomes;

◆ illustrations the student makes for the tales;

◆ replications of the visual organizers the class creates;

◆ sentences or pictures about favorite tales;

◆ results of cooperative learning and partner activities;

◆ lists of other folktales the student has enjoyed;

◆ plans for similar tales the student wishes to write;

◆ a glossary of words and phrases that the student likes.

Suggest that students work with partners to organize and make covers for their folders. Set aside conference time to go through portfolios with individual students. Discuss what they have learned about the tale-type, the tales they enjoyed most, their goals for their own tales, and various ways they might share the tales with classmates.

STUDENTS' OWN STORIES AS THEIR FINAL PRODUCTS

You'll probably find that your students are eager to write their own stories. Encourage students to talk about their stories and to keep ongoing phrase and picture lists of their ideas, to include these in their portfolios, and to begin writing their own tales as soon as they feel like it, reminding them that stories can always be revised. The student activity sheet that concludes each section provides a strategy for organizing and/or revising original stories.

In keeping with the oral tradition that is special to folktales, encourage students to share their stories by first telling them aloud or acting them out with classmates. You might plan a Folktale Day in which your students can tell and enact their stories for students in other classrooms. If possible, tape-record the tell-aloud stories and videotape the plays.

Students can put their written stories or picture-tales in a class Folktale Folder in addition to their portfolios for classmates to read and discuss independently. Finally, you may wish to make copies of students' stories for a Folktale Magazine that each student can bring home.

We think you'll find folk literature to be a delightful addition to your classroom. The tales here are old: In one way or another, they are part of your own heritage. But the presentation of these stories is new: In one volume you have the tales and the strategies to turn your students on to the fun and excitement of traditional stories and to the age-old human feelings, concerns, and understandings they evoke.

TRICKSTER TALES

CHARACTERISTICS OF TRICKSTER TALES

The protagonist of a trickster tale is a clever, devious animal whose pranks usually cause trouble for another character. In most instances, the trickster goes away gloating and unpunished, though in some tales there is a turnabout, and the trickster falls prey to the mischief he started.

Almost all traditional cultures tell stories featuring specific tricksters. For example, Coyote, Hare, or Raven are the featured tricksters across North America. West African trickster stories star Tortoise, Anansi the Spider, or Zomo the Hare (African storytellers brought the latter two to America, where Zomo eventually became Bre'r Rabbit). In Japan, the trickster is Badger, and in Europe and South and Central America he is Fox or Wolf.

What's the long-lasting appeal of a mischievous hero who so often gets away with causing trouble? One answer is that trickster stories make people laugh, just as practical jokers amuse some people today. A deeper reason for the popularity of tricksters is the way they combine mischief with creativity. Tricksters figure in the cosmology of many cultures, creating many features of the natural world as they play their pranks. An example is in the story "Coyote and the Wolves": In tricking the wolves, Coyote forms constellations in the night sky.

A third reason why trickster stories endure is that they also teach lessons about the futility of vanity, the perils of being naive about ways of the world, and the punishments that may come from being greedy. The butts of the trickster's jokes are often characters who exhibit these traits and who come away wiser after their encounters with him. For example, in "The Teapot Badger," greedy children learn a hard lesson about taking what belongs to another.

WHOLE-CLASS SECTION PROJECT

To help students grasp the sequence in trickster stories and to prepare them for writing trickster stories of their own, create a large oaktag Story Clock Organizer for the class to fill in after they discuss each tale. This example is based on the first tale, "Tortoise Tricks Leopard." Keep all the organizers on display for students to refer to as they compare and contrast the tales.

4. How does the story end? The squirrels think Leopard is Tortoise's horse.

1. Who is the Trickster? Tortoise

3. What is the trick? Tortoise says he has to ride on Leopard. He puts things on Leopard to make him seem like a horse.

2. Who gets tricked? Leopard

TORTOISE TRICKS LEOPARD

LIBERIAN

◆ **OBJECTIVE:** To become familiar with the major characteristics of trickster tales

◆ **STORY SUMMARY:** Tortoise tells his friends that Leopard is his horse. Leopard is indignant when the story is reported to him, and goes to Tortoise to get revenge. Tortoise denies the story, then tricks Leopard into acting like a horse.

SUGGESTED PROCEDURE

1. Read the story straight through for students to enjoy.

2. Discuss the trick that Tortoise played and the events that lead up to it: Tortoise told a lie, then became frightened of Leopard and told another lie to escape being eaten. After discussing the difficulties that telling falsehoods can get us into, talk about the characteristic that enabled Tortoise to win in the end: He is clever. Introduce the word *trickster* as the term we use for this kind of clever but dishonest character. Tales in which these characters appear are called trickster tales.

3. Discuss why Leopard fell for the trick: He is very *proud* and doesn't want his reputation ruined; he is very *foolish* not to realize that Tortoise is making him look like a horse.

4. Invite the class to fill in a Story Clock Organizer for this tale. Then distribute Activity Sheet 1 for students to complete in pairs. Suggest that partners use the cutouts and the organizer as they retell the tale to a small group of classmates.

FOLLOW-UP ACTIVITIES

1. Explain that the story characters are native to Liberia, which is where the story came from. Invite students to suggest animal characters if the tale were taking place in their own area. Encourage volunteers to tell aloud a local adaptation of the story.

2. Invite students to compare practical jokes (the kind of jokes tricksters play) to jokes in which everyone can laugh at the end, such as riddles or funny anecdotes. Practical jokes tend only to be funny to the person playing them, and the butt of the joke is often left feeling angry or embarrassed. Students can discuss which kind of joke they like best and why.

3. Invite small groups of students to act out the tale. Challenge them to find simple props in the classroom to represent the saddle blanket, the reins, and the fly switch.

Tortoise Tricks Leopard

Tortoise and his friend Gray Squirrel were sitting under a tree and talking. Gray Squirrel bragged about how fast he could run. Tortoise said, "I may walk slow, but I always ride in style! That's because Leopard is my horse!"

As soon as Tortoise went home, Gray Squirrel ran to Leopard and said, "I hear you are Tortoise's horse! Ho, ho! What a sight that must be! A powerful animal like you being tamed by Tortoise!"

Leopard was very angry. "I will eat that liar up," he growled to himself as he ran to Tortoise's burrow. Tortoise was frightened when Leopard burst into his home, his teeth all shiny and sharp.

"You miserable lump!" snarled Leopard. "How dare you tell Squirrel that I am your horse? What a ridiculous notion! I'm going to chew you up and gobble you down for spreading a tale like that!"

"Squirrel said *that*?" exclaimed Tortoise. "Why, I never told any such lie! Squirrel is telling tales, just so that he can break up our friendship. We must go to him right away and punish him."

Leopard looked puzzled. Then he said, "Well, all right. Let's go right away and have it out with Gray Squirrel."

"The only thing is," said Tortoise, "that I can't move as fast as you. It would take me all day to get to Squirrel's house. Of course, if you carried me on your back we would get there fast."

"All right," said Leopard. "Climb up on my back."

They went along that way for a while, until Tortoise fell off Leopard's back with a loud PLOP.

"Whatever is the matter?" asked Leopard.

"Your back is very sleek and glossy," explained Tortoise. "I just seem to slide right off. But perhaps if we put a seat on your back I can stay put."

"Oh, all right," agreed Leopard. Tortoise found a blanket at the side of the road. He folded it to make a seat, then climbed up again on Leopard's back. And off they went again.

But in a very little while again, PLOP... Tortoise fell off!

"*Now* what's wrong?" asked Leopard.

"Sorry about that," sighed Tortoise. "But I've got nothing to hold onto up here, and I keep losing my balance. But perhaps if we put a long piece of rope through your mouth, I could hold on to that."

"Oh, all right," grumbled Leopard. Tortoise found some rope hanging from a tree and fastened it through Leopard's mouth. And off they went again. But it wasn't long before Tortoise began to yell.

"OW, OW, OW!" he hollered. "Flies are biting me! Thousands of little flies! I need a switch to shoo them away! Please, stop by this tree so that I can get a little branch to use as a flyswatter."

"Oh, all right," grumbled Leopard. Tortoise picked himself a branch, and began to wave it about.

Now they came to Gray Squirrel's house, Tortoise sitting on a saddle-blanket and waving a switch, and Leopard with reins through his mouth.

"Look, look!" cried Gray Squirrel and all his family. "Leopard really is Tortoise's horse!" And the squirrels laughed and laughed. Tortoise jumped off Leopard's back and began to laugh, too. As for Leopard, he was so embarrassed that he ran away into the forest and stayed alone for a long time, pouting.

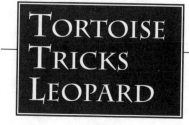
TORTOISE TRICKS LEOPARD

Trickster Tale Picture Story

Color the pictures and cut them out. Then get another sheet of paper. Paste the pictures to tell the story in order.

HARE TRICKS LION INDIAN

◆ **OBJECTIVE:** To compare characters in trickster tales

◆ **STORY SUMMARY:** The animals, in an attempt to keep Lion from destroying many of them each day, promise to send just one of their group to him as a daily meal. Hare volunteers to be the first sacrifice, then tricks Lion into believing that another lion has stolen other food that was on the way. Lion goes out to do battle with this fictitious rival. Seeing his reflection in a stream, he thinks he has met the enemy, dives in to attack him, and drowns.

SUGGESTED PROCEDURE

1. Read the story straight through.

2. Discuss Hare's motive for playing the trick and the characteristics of Lion that led him to fall for it (greed, anger). Invite students to compare Hare's lie in this tale and Tortoise's lie in "Tortoise Tricks Leopard": Is one lie more justifiable than the other? Is it okay to lie in order to save your life?

3. As students complete their Story Clock Organizers for this tale, have them compare and contrast the tricksters and their victims in the two stories they have now read. Which characters are small but smart? Which characters are large, powerful, and gullible?

4. Distribute and discuss Activity Sheet 2. Brainstorm a list of animals that fit into the two different categories. After students complete the activity, suggest that they include the page in their portfolio to refer to when writing their own trickster tales.

FOLLOW-UP ACTIVITIES

1. As a science activity, invite students to research facts about the animals in the trickster stories they've read. Introduce the activity by discussing how the story characters are made to seem like humans, with human faults and capabilities like speech. In real life, are leopards and lions really mean, vain, and foolish? What is their natural food? (They are carnivores.) How do they catch their prey?

2. Read the Aesop fable "The Dog and the Bone" (see Bibliography, page 111). Discuss the similarity between what happens to the dog in the fable and the lion in this tale. Invite students to make up a tell-aloud story about another animal who is tricked by a reflection.

Hare Tricks Lion

Lion had a ferocious appetite! Every day, he made fierce raids on the villages of other animals as he looked for someone to eat. He wrecked houses and scattered everyone far and wide as they went running for cover.

The animals held an emergency meeting to decide what to do. After much arguing and discussion, Old Hare had an idea.

"Why should we wait here trembling for Lion to come and destroy our villages?" said Old Hare. "Instead, we will send food to Lion. Each day, someone among us will generously volunteer to go to Lion's house and be Lion's meal for the day."

The animals thought that was an excellent idea. Not one of them volunteered, however.

"Come, come!" said Old Hare. "Is no one brave and generous enough to make the first noble sacrifice?"

There was dead silence. Finally Little Hare raised his hand. "I'll go," he said. "I'll be the first one."

All the other animals were greatly relieved and praised Little Hare for his courage. And off he went, into the forest.

When he came to Lion's house, Little Hare explained that he was volunteering to be a meal. "Now you won't have to raid the villages and scare everyone," said Little Hare.

Lion laughed alarmingly and showed his shiny teeth. "You must be joking!" he snarled. "Whatever makes you think that one little hare would be enough to satisfy me for the day? I need lots and lots of food, for breakfast, lunch, and dinner… and I need snacks, too!"

"Oh, but Lion," said Little Hare. "Many, many animals did set out with me to be your meal today. But I'm the only one left. You see, as we passed by the great river another huge lion jumped out and grabbed all the other volunteers and ate them. Only I escaped. He was a huge, great beast… more powerful than you, I think."

"*No* one is more powerful than I am!" roared Lion. "I'll show you how mighty I am. I'll find that sneaky beast who robbed me of my meal, and I'll devour *him*!"

Lion roared and raced through the forest and stopped by the edge of the great river. "Come out of hiding, you thief!" he bellowed, "or I'll come and find you." Lion paced angrily along the river bank, searching for his enemy. Finally, he looked into the water. There was the lion! He did look quite strong and fierce, staring back from the deep water.

"Come out, you coward, and fight like a lion!" said Lion.

The other lion stayed put.

"Well, then, since you aren't brave enough to come *out* and fight, I'll have to go *in* and fight," announced Lion. He jumped into the river and promptly drowned.

Little Hare had followed quietly behind, and laughed when he saw Lion's fate. He went home to his village and assured the other animals that they would be safe now, for Lion had been killed by his own reflection.

Trickster Tale Characters

Draw pictures to show other tricksters and other animals who get tricked.

Trebsters

| Tortoise | Hare | | |

Animals Who Get Tricked

| Leopard | Lion | | |

21

BRE'R RABBIT AND BRE'R FOX

AFRICAN-AMERICAN

◆ **OBJECTIVE:** To identify values in trickster tales

◆ **STORY SUMMARY:** Two tricksters collide in this story. Bre'r Rabbit plays a trick that enables him to drink up most of the milk Bre'r Fox has been saving. In retaliation for this theft, Bre'r Fox builds a sticky statue of a child out of tar, knowing that Bre'r Rabbit will think the statue real and expect the "child" to respond politely. When this doesn't happen, Bre'r Rabbit gets himself thoroughly stuck on the statue as he attempts to punish the unmannerly "child." Bre'r Fox captures his antagonist and threatens to cook him. The rabbit outwits the fox by begging not to be thrown into a briar patch. Bre'r Fox promptly does this, of course, and Bre'r Rabbit hops home.

SUGGESTED PROCEDURE

1. Ask students to listen to find out how many tricksters there are in this tale. Then read the story straight through.

2. Discuss what Bre'r Rabbit did that angered Bre'r Fox. (He stole milk.) Then discuss why Bre'r Rabbit first got angry at the sticky statue. (He thought it was an impolite child; a polite child would have answered him.) Explain that honesty and good manners are valued by most groups of people, and that sometimes their tales show what happens when these rules are broken.

FOLLOW-UP ACTIVITIES

1. Invite students to tell a chain-trickster tale of their own about Bre'r Fox and Bre'r Rabbit, using this one as a model and working in the same values of honesty and politeness.

2. After the class fills out the Story Clock Organizer for this tale, suggest that they use it as a guide to act out the story, using their stick puppets from Activity Sheet 3.

3. Begin a Trickster Tale Mural. Suggest that each cooperative-learning group choose one of the tales read so far and depict the characters on a section of the mural. Reserve room on the mural for showing the characters in the last two tales in this section.

BRE'R RABBIT AND BRE'R FOX

Brother Fox was building a house. He asked Brother Rabbit to help him. "Why, sure!" said Bre'r Rabbit. But he had no intention of helping. What he really wanted was a nice pail of milk that Bre'r Fox had standing by in a cool stream, for refreshment.

Every time Bre'r Fox started a hard part of the building job, like sawing logs or shingling the roof, Bre'r Rabbit said, "Oooh, whooo! I think I hear my dear little children calling me! I must go find out what they want." Then off he'd hop to get a big drink of milk. This happened a lot of times.

Bre'r Fox said, "I notice that when you go off to help your children, you don't come back til the hard work's done. I also notice that when I go to get a little refreshment to cool my tired self, the level of the milk has sunk considerably."

"Don't know a thing about it!" said Bre'r Rabbit. Then he said, "Oooh, whooo! I think I hear my dear little children calling me."

This time Bre'r Fox followed him secretly. He watched Bre'r Rabbit slurp up a lot of milk and take a little nap.

"That lazy rabbit!" said Bre'r Fox angrily. "I'll fix him! I know what a store he sets by children being polite!" Bre'r Fox took some tar from a pine tree and made a tar-statue that looked like a child. He set the Tar Baby by the side of the road near the milk. The next time Bre'r Rabbit pulled his "ooh, whoo" trick and went for the milk, he saw the Tar Baby. "Why, hello there, child," said Bre'r Rabbit. The Tar Baby didn't answer.

"Why, you rude little thing!" exclaimed Bre'r Rabbit. "You need a slap to remind you of your manners!" He slapped the Tar Baby with his front paws, and got them stuck in the sticky tar.

"Let me go, you un-mannerly kid!" said Bre'r Rabbit. He kicked the Tar Baby with his back paws. They, too, got stuck in the tar.

And there Bre'r Rabbit was stuck, ranting and shouting, when Bre'r Fox found him.

"Nothing will do for you but to take you back to my house and cook you for my supper," said Bre'r Fox, as he pulled Bre'r Rabbit loose from the sticky tar.

"Do as you like!" hollered Bre'r Rabbit. "Eat me if you wish. Just don't throw me in the briar patch. Please don't do *that*! Being thrown in the briar patch is a fate worse than being your supper!"

"Well," said Bre'r Fox. "I'm so angry at you for tricking me that I want you to have the worst possible fate. So it's the briar patch for you!" And, with a big laugh, he tossed Bre'r Rabbit into the thorny, brambly briar patch.

Bre'r Rabbit jumped away laughing. "Born and bred in a briar patch!" he hollered. "I was born and bred in a briar patch, Bre'r Fox!" And away he scampered.

BRE'R RABBIT AND BRE'R FOX

Tricky Stick Puppets

Paste the page on heavy paper. Color the characters and cut them out. Glue or tape them to strips of cardboard or tongue depressors to make stick puppets. Use your puppets to tell the story.

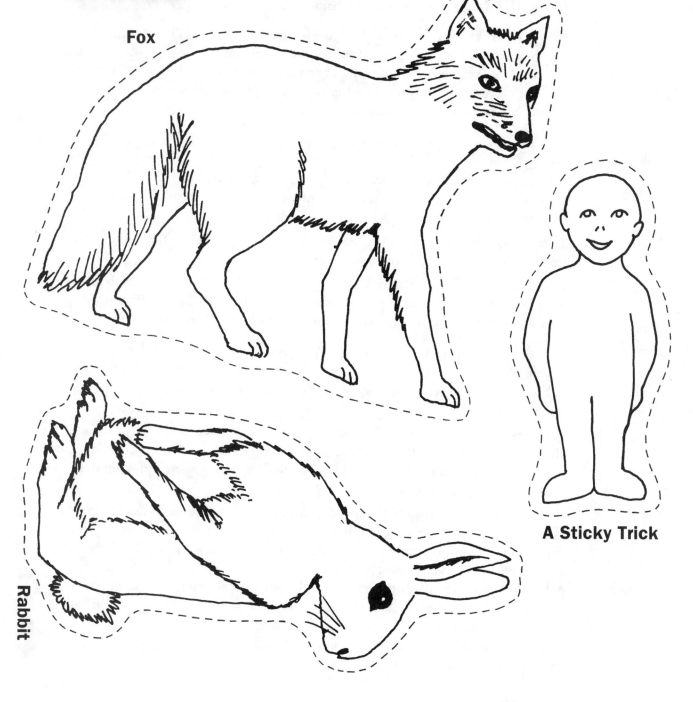

Fox

A Sticky Trick

Rabbit

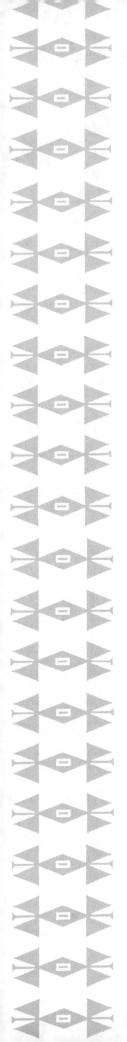

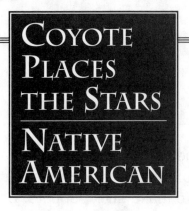
◆ **OBJECTIVE:** To predict what will happen in a trickster tale

◆ **STORY SUMMARY:** Coyote is friends with five wolves who are brothers. The wolves spot two animals way up in the sky. One day, Coyote builds a ladder, and the wolves climb it. Then Coyote dismantles the ladder, stranding the wolves in the heavens. Like the two animals (who turn out to be bears), the wolves become stars and can be seen even now.

SUGGESTED PROCEDURE

1. Read the title and invite students to tell who the story's trickster is and how they know. Encourage children to predict what the story is about. Record their predictions on chart paper.

2. Pause after the part of the story in which Coyote builds a ladder to the sky and ask students to make new predictions about what will happen next.

3. After students fill in the Story Clock Organizer for this tale, invite them to retell the story in cooperative groups. If your students have read any "Why" stories, such as the ones on pages 55-76, invite them to tell how this trickster tale is also a "Why" story.

FOLLOW-UP ACTIVITIES

1. Invite students to retell the story of "Coyote Places the Stars" by completing Activity Sheet 4.

2. Have students find constellation pictures in encyclopedias and in library books about stars. Students can then use black construction paper and white crayons or paint to replicate various constellations and label them. Display the star pictures on the classroom ceiling or along windows.

3. If possible, arrange for a field trip to a planetarium so that students can find out about the Bear constellations and other constellations. Discuss how people in earlier cultures had many opportunities to sit outside at night, look at the stars, and make up stories about animals and people they imagined in the stars. As a classroom activity, pull down the shades, turn off the lights, and invite your storytellers to sit in a circle and tell their own stories about make-believe sky characters based on the constellation pictures they've seen.

4. A cooperative learning group can add characters from this story to the Trickster Tale Mural (see page 22).

COYOTE PLACES THE STARS

BY BARRY LOPEZ

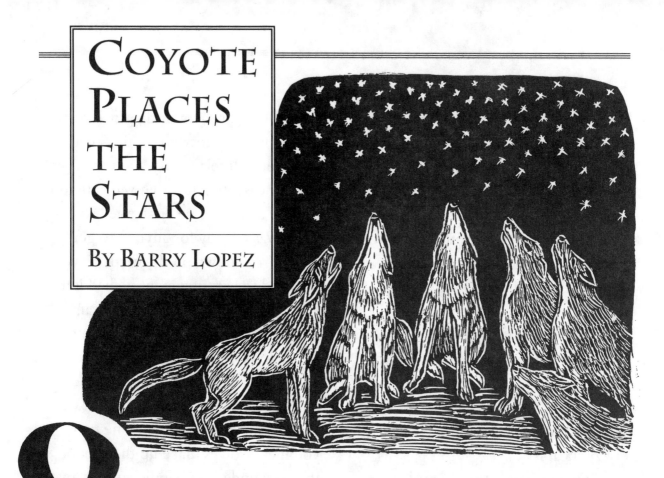

One time there were five wolves, all brothers, who traveled together. Whatever meat they got when they were hunting they would share with Coyote. One evening Coyote saw the wolves looking up at the sky.

"What are you looking at up there, my brothers?" asked Coyote.

"Oh, nothing," said the oldest wolf.

Next evening Coyote saw they were all looking up in the sky at something. He asked the next oldest wolf what they were looking at, but he wouldn't say. It went on like this for three or four nights. No one wanted to tell Coyote what they were looking at because they thought he would want to interfere. One night Coyote asked the youngest wolf brother to tell him and the youngest wolf said to the other wolves, "Let's tell Coyote what we see up there. He won't do anything."

So they told him. "We see two animals up there. Way up there, where we cannot get to them."

"Let's go up and see them," said Coyote.

"Well, how can we do that?"

"Oh, I can do that easy," said Coyote. "I can show you how to get up there without any trouble at all."

Coyote gathered a great number of arrows and then began shooting them into the sky. The first arrow stuck in the sky and then the second arrow stuck in the first. Each arrow stuck in the end of the one before it like that until there was a ladder reaching down to the earth.

"We can climb up now," said Coyote. The oldest wolf took his dog with him, and then the other four wolf brothers came, and then Coyote. They climbed all day and into the night. All the next day they climbed. For many days and nights they climbed until finally they reached the sky. They stood in the sky and looked over at the two animals the wolves had seen from down below. They were two grizzly bears.

"Don't go near them," said Coyote. "They will tear you apart." But the two youngest wolves were already heading over. And the next two youngest wolves followed them. Only the oldest wolf held back. When the wolves got near the grizzlies, nothing happened. The wolves sat down and looked at the bears, and the bears sat there looking at the wolves. The oldest wolf, when he saw it was safe, came over with his dog and sat down with them.

Coyote wouldn't come over. He didn't trust bears. "That makes a nice picture, though," thought Coyote. "They all look pretty good sitting there like that. I think I'll leave it that way for everyone to see. Then when people look at them in the sky they will say, 'There's a story about that picture,' and they will tell a story about me."

So Coyote left it that way. He took out the arrows as he descended so there was no way for anyone to get back. From down on the earth Coyote admired the arrangement he had left there. Today they still look the same. They call those stars Big Dipper now. If you look up there you'll see three wolves make up the handle and the oldest wolf, the one in the middle, still has his dog with him. The two youngest wolves make up the part of the bow under the handle and the two grizzlies make up the other side, the one that points toward the North Star.

When Coyote saw how they looked, he wanted to put up a lot of stars. He arranged stars all over the sky in pictures and then made the Big Road across the sky with the stars he had left over.

When Coyote was finished, he called Meadowlark over. "My brother," he said, "When I am gone, tell everyone that when they look up into the sky and see the stars arranged this way, that I was the one who did that. This is my work."

Now Meadowlark tells that story. About Coyote.

COYOTE PLACES THE STARS

A Starry Story

Finish the picture to answer these questions.

1. How do the wolves get to the sky?

2. What are the wolves looking at?

3. Who sings the story about Coyote and the wolves?

Use your picture to tell the story to a classmate.

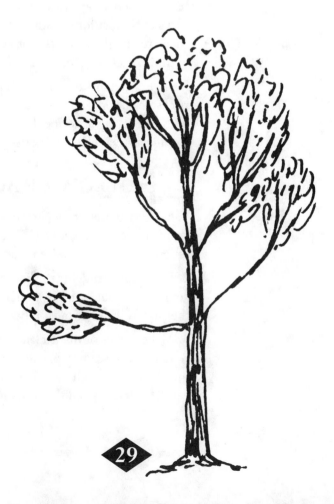

THE TEAPOT BADGER

JAPANESE

◆ **OBJECTIVE:** To write a trickster tale

◆ **STORY SUMMARY:** A poor old man is renown for his kindness to children. To reward him, Badger turns himself into a magic teapot which will brew delicious tea without need of leaves or water. Some of the old man's students try to steal the teapot, but it changes back into Badger and scares them away. His identity revealed, Badger suggests to the old man that they perform the teapot-Badger trick for audiences. The old man does so, and becomes rich.

SUGGESTED PROCEDURE

1. Review the organizers and discuss how all the characters in the trickster tales students have read are animals. Explain that this tale has an animal trickster and human characters, too. Invite students to suggest pranks that tricksters might play on humans. Then read the story straight through.

2. After students fill in the Story Clock Organizer for this tale, discuss what they have learned about trickster tales; for example: The main character is an animal who plays tricks just for fun; the other character or characters fall for the trick because they are greedy or foolish, or are also tricksters; often the main trickster gets away with the trick, but sometimes he, too, is fooled.

3. Invite students to work with partners or in small groups to write their own trickster tales. As an alternative, the class can work together to create a trickster tale, with you acting as scribe. Distribute copies of Activity Sheet 5 for students to use as a guide as they plan and write their tales.

FOLLOW-UP ACTIVITIES

1. Suggest that writing partners or writing groups illustrate their trickster tales, title them, and make cover pages listing the authors' names. Or, if the class writes the tale together, suggest that each student copy all or part of the story and illustrate it.

2. Encourage students to share their stories by reading or telling them aloud, or by acting them out. Ask the audience to listen for and discuss the elements that make the story a trickster tale. Tape-record the stories and skits.

3. Make copies of the trickster tales to keep in a Folktale Folder in the reading center. Invite reading partners to read the stories, listen to the tape, and discuss what they like about each tale. Then have students complete the Trickster Tale Mural with characters from this story and their own stories (see page 22).

THE TEAPOT BADGER

There was once a poor old man who was kind to everyone, especially to children. He told them stories, taught them how to paint pictures and write, and shared whatever little bits of food he managed to grow in his garden.

"That is a fine old man!" said Badger. "I think I will reward him for his kindness."

Badger went to the old man's house and turned himself into a teapot full of delicious tea. When the old man found the teapot, he was very much surprised and happy, for he had never been able to afford a teapot. And when he looked into the teapot and saw that it was full, he was even more surprised, for he had never been able to afford tea leaves. And when he drank the tea, he was astonished! This must be the best-tasting tea in all the world! And surprise of surprises… no matter how much tea the old man drank, the teapot was always full.

In the evening, three children came to the old man's garden. "Tell us a story!" they pleaded.

"I'll tell you a *true* story, today," said the man. And he told the children about the magic teapot. When the story was done, he went to the orchard to pick some fruit for his young guests.

While the old man was gone, the children said, "Let's go into the house and take the magic teapot."

The children crept into the house. There was the teapot sitting on a table. But just as the oldest child reached for it, the pot turned back into Badger.

His long teeth flashing and his tail waving in anger, Badger chased after the thieves, nipping at their heels and growling fiercely. The children fled from the house screaming and hollering, while Badger laughed and laughed.

"Whatever is the matter?" called the old man from the orchard.

"Your teapot is really Badger!" sobbed the children. "Look here, where he nipped our feet!"

"How can a teapot be Badger?" said the old man. He went into his house. There was the teapot, the same as ever. The man came out and said to the children, "Surely you were dreaming!" Then he went back to the orchard.

The children took big sticks and sneaked back into the house. They began to beat the teapot and pour hot water on it. The pot turned back into Badger. "Never, never mistreat me!" he snarled. And he leapt from the table and chased the frightened children all through the house as they screamed and hollered.

Badger thought it was very funny to see them hop around like that. "What do you expect when you try to steal things?" he laughed as he nipped at their heels.

The old man came hobbling in from the orchard to see what all the commotion was about. How alarmed he was to see Badger chasing his little friends! He took up a stick to hit Badger with.

"Uh, uh! Never beat me, never mistreat me!" said Badger. He told the old man all about what had happened. The children got very red in the face with shame.

"This house is no place for me," said Badger finally. "Here is what we'll do, old man. You and I shall travel on the roads together and give shows along the way. It will be a magic show. You will show me as teapot, and then I'll change into Badger, and then back into a teapot. People will give you many gold coins to see this wonderful trick."

This is the way the old man finally became rich. Then he came back home and put the teapot in a little temple on the top of the hill in his orchard. It was greatly honored there, especially by the children who had once tried to steal it.

Trickster Tale Writing Plan

Write your plans for a trickster tale on the chart below.
Use your answers to help you write your trickster tale.

Who is the trickster?
Who gets tricked?
What is the trick?
What happens at the end?
What is the title of this trickster tale?

FABLES

CHARACTERISTICS OF FABLES

Fables are brief stories told to teach specific lessons, or morals.

While many fables feature anthropomorphized (humanized) animal characters, as in "The Mice and the Cat" and "The Lion and the Mouse," many others have human protagonists, as in "The Shepherd Boy."

Aesop, supposedly a Greek slave who lived and taught in Asia Minor about 600 B.C., told many of the fables most familiar to us today.

Over the centuries, storytellers in Africa and Europe adapted these fables to their particular geographic settings, while keeping the essential morals intact. Aesop's morals, stated at the end of the tale, usually have to do with using one's wits to overcome enemies or to achieve some practical, worldly purpose.

Fables from India, like the Jataka tales (recorded about 500 B.C.), represent Eastern cultures and philosophies. These fables stress such themes as the value of cooperation, the wisdom of looking at problems from different viewpoints, and the rewards of being satisfied with what life deals you. Indian fables usually have several layers of meaning. For this reason, the morals are not stated directly. The listener is challenged to talk about the tale and thus find his or her own lesson in it.

WHOLE-CLASS SECTION PROJECT

To help students grasp the structure of fables and to prepare them for writing fables of their own, create a large oaktag Fables Chart Organizer. As each new tale is read, invite students to fill in the chart by drawing pictures and/or writing descriptions of the characters and events in the story. The entry below is based on the first story in this section, "The Mice and the Cat." Hang the chart so students can refer to it when they read the stories in this section.

Title	Characters	Problem	Action	Moral
The Mice and the Cat	mice young mouse old mouse cat	How to keep safe from the cat	A little mouse says put a bell. No mouse will do it.	Ideas that don't work are not worth anything.

THE MICE AND THE CAT
AESOP

◆ **OBJECTIVE:** To become familiar with the major characteristics of fables

◆ **STORY SUMMARY:** In this fable, from which comes the saying "belling the cat," a young mouse proposes putting a bell around the cat's neck as an early-warning system for possible mouse victims. Of course, no mouse volunteers to carry out the plan.

SUGGESTED PROCEDURE

1. Explain that you are going to read a story called a *fable*, and that a fable is a very short story that ends with a lesson, or *moral*. Then read the story straight through.

2. Discuss the story ending to make sure students understand *why* none of the mice volunteer to put a collar on the cat and why the young mouse's idea thus won't work. Invite volunteers to tell about their own experiences with ideas that didn't work because they were impossible to carry out.

3. Display the Fables Chart Organizer (page 35) and guide students as they suggest ways to fill it in for this tale.

4. Distribute copies of Activity Sheet 6 for students to use as they retell the story in their own way. Some students may wish to copy the moral from the Fables Chart Organizer at the bottom of the page.

5. Suggest that students make Fable Portfolios to hold this activity sheet and other fables they will read and create.

FOLLOW-UP ACTIVITIES

1. Cooperative-learning groups can act out the fable, with embellishments of their own. For example, three or four members can think up other solutions the mice might offer as they plan how to outwit the cat. One member can play the role of cat as it first scatters or pounces on the mice and later laughs at and comments on the young mouse's idea. Members playing the old mouse and the young mouse can develop distinct voices for these characters.

2. Invite students to draw picture-fables that have the same moral and general problem but use different casts of characters, for example, cats that wish to escape from dogs, worms that wish to escape from birds, or deer that wish to escape from hunters. After students have shared their stories with the class, they can include them in their portfolios.

THE MICE AND THE CAT

The mice once held a meeting to decide what to do about the cat. The cat made their lives miserable. He was always sneaking up among them and eating one of their number.

Though the mice talked for hours, not one of them could think of

a solution to the problem. Finally a young mouse spoke up.

"I know what we can do!" he said. "The trouble with the cat is that he is so quiet. We have no warning about when he is coming. So let's get a small bell, put it on a collar, and tie it around the cat's neck. Whenever we hear the bell, we can run for cover."

The other mice were delighted with this idea. They praised the young mouse for his cleverness and wished they had thought of the idea themselves.

But then an old mouse asked, "And which of us will volunteer to approach the cat and tie a bell on him?"

The mice fell silent. Not one of them volunteered to bell the cat.

Moral: Ideas that won't work are not worth anything.

THE MICE AND THE CAT

Retelling the Fable in Pictures

Retell the story using these pictures. Then write the moral below.

1.

2.

3.

4. Who will do it?

Moral: _____

_____

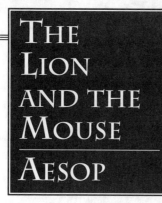

THE LION AND THE MOUSE
AESOP

◆ **OBJECTIVE:** To understand the purpose of a fable

◆ **STORY SUMMARY:** A lion spares the life of a mouse, but laughs at the idea that the mouse can return the favor. Later, the mouse *does* return the favor by freeing the lion from a hunter's net.

SUGGESTED PROCEDURE

1. Tell students the moral of this fable first. ("An act of kindness always comes back to you.") Then read the story straight through for students to enjoy.

2. Discuss the ways in which the lion and the mouse were kind. Get students' opinions as to how the fable proves the moral. Invite students to tell how their own kind acts or the kind acts of others toward them were repaid.

3. After students have entered the data for this fable on the Fables Chart Organizer, distribute copies of Activity Sheet 7. Invite reading partners to use the sheet to retell the story to one another. Explain that in the blank frame they can draw their own picture of how the mouse repays the lion's kindness.

4. Ask students to include the activity sheet in their portfolios.

FOLLOW-UP ACTIVITIES

1. Invite student partners to plan and enact the fable and its moral using two animals native to their own region as characters. Introduce the activity by pointing out on a map or globe where the original teller of the tale (Aesop) lived (on the western Asian peninsula between the Black Sea and the Mediterranean) and explaining that he used animals native to that area as characters. Then invite the class to make two lists of local animals: one of strong or large animals, and another of small animals. Partners can choose one animal from each list to portray in their skits. Encourage the audience to discuss how the actors proved the moral of the story in their play.

2. Discuss other stories the class has read in which characters are rewarded for their kindness. For example, in John Steptoe's *The Story of Jumping Mouse* (see Bibliography, page 109), the hero gives up his senses to other animals that are in need and is rewarded by becoming an eagle. Invite students to make a class mural illustrating acts of kindness they have read or heard about.

THE LION AND THE MOUSE

One day a lion lay sleeping peacefully in the sun. Quite by mistake, a small mouse ran right over the lion's nose. The lion woke with a start and clapped his huge paw over the mouse.

"My, what a nice little snack *you* will make," roared the lion.

"Oh, please sir," said the mouse, "spare my life! I didn't mean to disturb you. Please let me go! I was only out looking for seeds for my hungry children."

"What do I care about your children?" said the lion. "I'm hungry, too!" And he opened his big jaws.

"Mercy!" cried the mouse. "If you let me go, I will do a kind deed for you someday."

The lion laughed. "And how do you think a tiny little creature like you can help a mighty creature like me? That's the funniest thing I ever heard. But I'll let you go because you make me laugh, which is something I seldom do."

The lion lifted his paw and the grateful mouse scurried away.

A few days later, the mouse was gathering seeds again when she heard a terrible, sad roaring in the distance. "That's the lion!" said the mouse, and she scampered toward the sound. She found the lion trapped under a huge net that hunters had set to trap lions.

"Woe is me!" cried the lion when he saw the mouse. "Soon the hunters will come back and kill me!"

"Never fear!" said the mouse. "I will free you." She set to work gnawing at the net with her sharp teeth. Soon she had made a large hole through which the lion could escape.

"You see?" said the mouse. "I told you I would repay you, small as I am."

Moral: An act of kindness always comes back to you.

A Picture-Perfect Fable

Draw a picture in frame 4 to show how the story ends.
Then write the moral below.

1.

2.

3.

4.

Moral: _____

_____

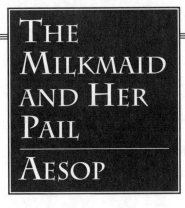

THE MILKMAID AND HER PAIL
AESOP

◆ **OBJECTIVE:** To relate fables to everyday life

◆ **STORY SUMMARY:** A milkmaid plans what she will do with the money she gets for her pail of milk. The milk spills, and all the milkmaid's plans are for naught.

SUGGESTED PROCEDURE

1. Tell students about a plan you made once that failed because something unexpected happened. An example is saving money for a special treat and then finding that you must spend the money for a sudden necessity. Invite volunteers to tell about similar experiences. Ask students to listen to the fable to find out about another person who planned too far ahead.

2. Pause after you come to the end of the second paragraph and invite students to predict what will happen next. Encourage them to give reasons for their predictions, then read the rest of the story.

3. After students have entered the data for this fable on the Fables Chart Organizer, distribute copies of Activity Sheet 8 and discuss pictures or words that can go in the frames. Invite students to work with a writing or drawing partner to complete their maps. Suggest that students add their maps to their portfolios.

FOLLOW-UP ACTIVITIES

1. Invite students to take turns reenacting the fable. Use a large plastic pail (empty!) for the actor to balance on her or his head as she or he walks across the playing area and plans aloud what to do with the money gained for the milk. Encourage actors to think of their own ways of spending the money.

2. To help students build an understanding of figurative language, discuss the lesson the milkmaid learned ("Don't count your chickens before they are hatched") and ways it could be "translated" for everyday use, such as, "Don't count on your plans working too far ahead of time." You might also review the story and moral in "The Mice and the Cat" and invite students to suggest translations of the phrase "belling the cat," such as, "setting up an impossible task."

3. Encourage pairs of students to write and answer "Dear Problem-Solver" letters based on fables they have read. For example, the lion in "The Lion and the Mouse" might ask: "A mouse wants me to set him free. Do you think I should?" One student from each pair can write the questions; the other student can write the answers. Students can illustrate their question-and-answer letters and display them on a bulletin board.

The Milkmaid and Her Pail

A milkmaid once walked along the path to the town, carrying a pail of milk on her head. As she walked she thought, "When I get to town, I will sell this milk. With the money I get, I will buy a fine hen. Of course, I won't eat the hen. I'll keep the hen safe while it lays plenty of eggs. And I won't eat the eggs either! I'll let them hatch into chicks."

The milkmaid went on with her plans as she came near the village. She thought, "When the chicks are grown, I'll take them to this village and sell each one. With the money I get for the chicks, I will buy a fine gown and ribbons to wear in my hair."

The milkmaid imagined how fine she would look in her new clothes. "Everyone will admire me," she thought. And with that, she gave a little toss of her head to show how she would walk proudly among her friends.

But when she tossed her head, the pail of milk fell off it, and all the milk was spilled on the ground.

Moral: Don't count your chickens before they are hatched.

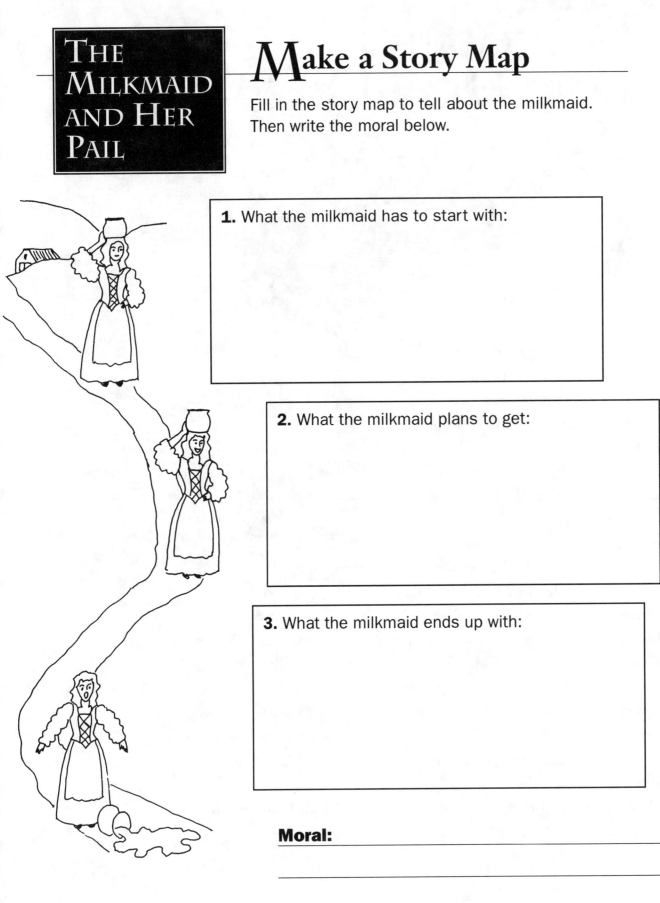

THE MILKMAID AND HER PAIL

Make a Story Map

Fill in the story map to tell about the milkmaid. Then write the moral below.

1. What the milkmaid has to start with:

2. What the milkmaid plans to get:

3. What the milkmaid ends up with:

Moral: _____

_____

THE SHEPHERD BOY

AESOP

◆ **OBJECTIVE:** To think critically about fable characters

◆ **STORY SUMMARY:** A shepherd boy grows bored and plays a trick on his neighbors by crying "Wolf!" when no wolf is around. When the wolf really does appear, the neighbors ignore the boy's cries because they think he is fooling them again.

SUGGESTED PROCEDURE

1. Introduce the fable by explaining that it is about a boy who plays a trick. Ask students to listen to find out what the trick is and how it turns out in the end.

2. Pause after the paragraph describing the farmers' reactions the first time they realize they have been tricked. Discuss the boy's motives for playing the trick and encourage students to give their opinions about his behavior. For whom was the trick fun? Why did the farmers grumble?

3. Repeat the procedure from Question 2 when you finish reading about the second time the trick is played. Ask students to predict what might happen if the boy plays the trick again. Then read the story conclusion and discuss the moral. What has the boy learned? Why didn't the farmers believe him the third time he cried "Wolf!"? Do you think the moral is true for everybody or just for the shepherd boy?

4. After entering the data on the Fables Chart Organizer, distribute copies of Activity Sheet 9. Invite reading or drawing partners to complete the frames to show what happened the three times the boy cried "Wolf!" Ask students to put their finished stories in their portfolios.

FOLLOW-UP ACTIVITIES

1. Invite cooperative-learning groups to act out the fable, adding their own dialogue for the shepherd, the farmers, and the wolf. Suggest that girls as well as boys can play the shepherd role, since women often tended sheep.

2. Discuss the differences between genuine tricks—those performed for an audience by magicians, jugglers, and clowns—and tricks that are essentially lies and are meant to upset, deceive, or frighten people. Which kind of trick is fun for those on the receiving end as well as for the performer? Invite volunteers to tell about their experiences with both kinds of tricks. For which kind of trick do people respond, "Oh, she is only crying 'Wolf!'"?

THE SHEPHERD BOY

A shepherd boy had the job of taking the sheep to their grassy pasture each day and guarding them from wolves who might eat them.

It was an easy job. The boy sat among the rocks and played his flute as he watched the sheep.

One day the shepherd boy became bored. To liven things up, he decided to play a trick on the farmers who were his neighbors.

"Wolf! Wolf!" cried the boy in a scared voice.

"We must save the sheep! We must help the shepherd boy!" the farmers shouted as they ran to the pasture.

"I fooled you! I fooled you!" laughed the shepherd boy. Grumbling, the farmers went home.

The next day, the shepherd boy played the same trick. He cried, "Wolf! Wolf!" and laughed to see his neighbors leaving their work behind and running up the hill to help.

"Fooled you again!" laughed the boy. Grumbling, the farmers went home.

But the very next day, a wolf really did come to the pasture and began to chase and eat the sheep.

"Wolf! Wolf!" hollered the frightened boy, for he couldn't fight the wolf off alone.

His neighbors heard him shouting, but said to one another, "Let's not pay any attention. It's only the silly shepherd boy trying to trick us again." And they went on with their plowing.

So the wolf ate well that day.

Moral: A liar will not be believed, even when he tells the truth.

Picture This!

Draw pictures to show what happened each time.
Then write the moral below.

The first time:

The second time:

The third time:

Moral: _____

_____

THE FOX AND THE DRUM

INDIAN

- ◆ **OBJECTIVE:** To infer the moral of a fable
- ◆ **STORY SUMMARY:** A fox sees a drum hanging from a tree and figures that the drum must be something to eat. After enjoying the drum sounds for a while, the fox's hunger takes over. He attacks the drum, rips it open, and of course finds nothing at all inside.

SUGGESTED PROCEDURE

1. Review the morals listed on the Fable Chart Organizer and point out that these morals are stated at the end of the stories. Explain that in this fable the moral is *not* stated. It's up to the listener or reader to figure out what the moral might be. Sometimes there is more than one moral. Ask students to listen as you read the story straight through.

2. Discuss the fox's feelings about the drum (he liked its sounds, and he also wanted to eat it) and what happened when he tried to do the latter. Invite students to brainstorm several morals for the story and write their ideas on the chalkboard. Accept a variety of responses. Examples: Don't eat strange foods. Don't destroy something that makes you happy. Always find out what something *is* before you decide what to do with it. Ask the class to choose the two or three morals that they think fit the story best. Copy these onto the Fable Chart Organizer along with other data for the tale.

3. Distribute copies of Activity Sheet 10. Invite writing partners to make up captions for the three pictures and write a moral at the bottom of the page.

FOLLOW-UP ACTIVITIES

1. This is a good story for partners to act out. One student can be the fox and the other can be the drum, using percussion instruments from your rhythm band.

2. Invite students to work in groups of three or four to identify a moral in another story or book they have read. For example, from *The Velveteen Rabbit* students might learn that "you will always be real to someone who loves you." From chapters of *Winnie-the-Pooh*, they might infer the moral "true friends help you in times of trouble." Invite the groups to present the moral to the class as the beginning of a guessing game. Have them give additional clues until the audience guesses the story title.

THE FOX AND THE DRUM

A fox went walking in the forest one day, and in the distance he heard a RATTA-TAT, BOOM-BOOM, RATTA-TAT sound. Now, this sound was made by a drum that someone had left hanging in a tree. Whenever the wind blew, the tree branches RATTA-TATTED on it. And whenever the drum hit the tree trunk, it went BOOM!

Now like most foxes, *this* fox had no idea what a *drum* was. So when he saw it hanging there, he thought it must be something to eat. After all, it was big, and it seemed to live on a tree, and it was covered with some kind of skin, and it made a noise.

The fox sat and watched the drum for a while. He began to very much like the sounds that it made. It made him want to dance and tap his feet and clap. But then another sound took over. It was the GRUMBLE-RUMBLE of the fox's tummy. It was time for him to eat this strange creature.

With his mouth watering, the fox leapt at the drum and ripped the skin off it. But of course there was nothing inside at all, just air. The fox was very disappointed. He was still hungry, and there were no more interesting noises to cheer him up.

Write All About It

Write what is happening in each picture to retell the story of "The Fox and the Drum." Then write the moral below.

1. _____

_____

_____

_____

2. _____

_____

_____

_____

3. _____

_____

_____

_____

Moral: _____

_____

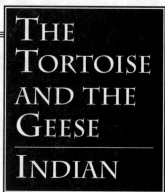

THE TORTOISE AND THE GEESE

INDIAN

◆ **OBJECTIVE:** To write a fable

◆ **STORY SUMMARY:** Two geese offer to take their friend, a tortoise, with them as they fly from a lake that has dried up to another lake high in the mountains. The geese will hold a stick between them with their bills, and the tortoise will clamp his jaws tightly around it during the flight. The geese warn their friend not to open his mouth, or he will fall. Midway in the journey, some children far below mock the "flying tortoise." He forgets the geese's warning, shouts back a retort, and falls to earth.

SUGGESTED PROCEDURE

1. Explain that this fable is like "The Fox and the Drum" in that listeners must figure out the moral for themselves. Then read the story straight through. Follow the procedure in Step 2 on page 48 as you discuss the story. Possible morals are: Sometimes it's best to keep silent. Don't try to fly if you can only walk. Don't go on dangerous journeys.

2. After students have filled in the Fables Chart Organizer with their suggested morals and other data from this tale, discuss what they have learned about fables: Fables are very short stories that teach a lesson; sometimes the lesson is stated at the end, and sometimes it is not; fables may have human characters or animal characters who talk and act like humans.

3. Invite students to work with a partner or small group to write their own fables, or suggest that the class work together to create a fable, with you acting as scribe. Suggest different procedures for the writers to choose from: selecting a moral from the Fables Chart Organizer and building a new tale that teaches the moral; or thinking of a new moral and making up a story to go with it. In the latter case, you may wish to discuss morals like these: If you try to please everyone, you will please no one; Better to work slowly than to work carelessly; Gentleness wins more friends than force does.

4. Distribute copies of Activity Sheet 11 for students to use as they plan their fables.

FOLLOW-UP ACTIVITIES

1. Suggest that students share their fables by illustrating them and reading them aloud, or by acting them out for the class. Invite the audience to identify the fable elements.

2. Have students include their original fables in their portfolios. Make copies of them for a reading-table folder.

THE TORTOISE AND THE GEESE

An old tortoise once lived by a lake, surrounded by his friends the geese. The tortoise was a talkative fellow who told many lively tales from morning 'til night. The geese thought he actually talked more than *they* did, which was quite a bit!

One year the rains failed to come and the lake began to dry up. "We must fly away from here!" said the geese. "We will fly to the Faraway Mountains, where the lakes are always full."

"But you can't leave me behind!" said the Tortoise. "I need water, too! Please take me with you!"

The geese thought about how they might do this, and finally hit on an idea.

"Now listen, Tortoise," they said. "We will carry this long, strong stick between us with our bills. You clamp your jaws tightly around the stick. Then we will carry you upward with us and off to the Faraway Mountains. But be warned: If you open your mouth, you will fall to Earth. And we know how hard it is for you to keep your mouth closed."

"I can do it! I can do it!" said the Tortoise.

So the Tortoise clamped his strong jaws around the stick and was borne aloft by the geese. How beautiful the flight was! Down below, the Tortoise could see fields and rivers, and far in the distance he could see the shimmery tops of the Faraway Mountains. When he looked down again, he could see a village below him.

Many children were playing outside, and when they looked up and saw the tortoise, they began to laugh and point. "Look at that silly tortoise!" they cried. "Did you ever see anything so ridiculous as a flying tortoise?"

"What do you mean, *silly*?" said the Tortoise. "How dare you laugh at me!" But of course when he opened his mouth to say this, he lost his grip on the stick. Down he fell to Earth, as the geese went on to the Faraway Mountains.

Writing a Fable

Fill in the chart below to plan your fable.
Then use it to write a story.

PLANS FOR MY FABLE
My fable characters:
The problem in my fable:
The main actions in my fable:
What happens at the end?:

"WHY" STORIES AND LEGENDS

CHARACTERISTICS OF "WHY" STORIES

"Why" stories present fanciful explanations of why animals look or behave as they do. The animals speak and have human personalities, problems, and motives. Generally, the tales have a humorous tone. The tellers and their audiences understand that the stories are meant primarily for entertainment.

Most "why" stories have characteristics that link them with fables or trickster tales. For example, in "Why Chickens and Hawks Are Enemies," there is an imbedded moral about the consequences of breaking a promise. In "Why Rabbit Has Long Ears and a Short Tail," the action begins with Fox playing a trick on Rabbit.

CHARACTERISTICS OF LEGENDS

While legends, too, tell about beginnings or changes in natural phenomena, they are more serious, for they deal with the proper relationships between humans and the natural environment. For example, the Papago legend "How Butterflies Came to Be" emphasizes the human need for beauty; the New Guinea legend "How Flying Fish Came to Be" stresses human responsibility for wisely using natural resources.

WHOLE-CLASS SECTION PROJECT

To help students grasp the structure of "why" stories and legends, and to prepare them for writing tales of their own, create a large oaktag Story Stair Organizer. As each new story is read, fill in the "steps" of the chart with key events in the story. Then invite children to draw pictures of those events. The entry below is based on the first story in this section, "Why Rabbit Has Long Ears and a Short Tale." Hang the charts around the room for students to refer to as they read the stories in this section.

1. What Rabbit looks like at the beginning

2. What Fox gets Rabbit to do

3. How Owl helps Rabbit

4. What Rabbit looks like at the end of the story

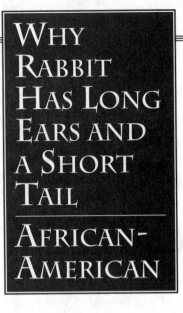

WHY RABBIT HAS LONG EARS AND A SHORT TAIL

AFRICAN-AMERICAN

◆ **OBJECTIVE:** To introduce "why" stories

◆ **STORY SUMMARY:** Tricked by Brother Fox, Brother Rabbit tries to catch fish by submerging his long tail in a pond. The pond freezes over and traps Rabbit. Brother Owl pulls Rabbit free by tugging on his short ears, which makes them long. Rabbit's long tail snaps off as he breaks free of the ice.

SUGGESTED PROCEDURE

1. Read the story straight through.

2. Discuss the phenomenon the story explains and invite students to tell how they know the story is "just for fun."

3. Discuss the three characters in the story and invite students to list words and phrases that describe them. For example, Fox is tricky and a liar. Rabbit is boastful and gullible. Owl is helpful. Then display the Story Stair Organizer and invite volunteers to draw pictures in each section to go with the labels. Students can refer to the stair as they take turns retelling the story in sequence.

FOLLOW-UP ACTIVITIES

1. Invite trios of students to act out the fable, adding whatever dialog they please. Suggest that the audience watch and listen to ascertain whether all episodes on the Story Stair Organizer are covered.

2. Cooperative-learning groups can make up their own stories about other ways in which Rabbit got long ears and a short tail. Suggest that group members act out each episode while a spokesperson shows the pictures in sequence and tells the story to the class.

3. Distribute and discuss Activity Sheet 12. After students have shown their finished work to classmates, suggest that they put the pages they have created into their portfolios.

Why Rabbit Has Long Ears and a Short Tail

A long time ago, Brother Rabbit didn't look like he does now. No, indeed! Rabbit had short ears and a long fluffy tail.

Rabbit was especially proud of that long tail. He was always showing it off to Brother Fox. "Look here!" Rabbit would say, "My tail is much longer and fluffier than your tail, Fox!" Brother Fox got very tired of all this bragging. "I wish I could find a way to keep Brother Rabbit from showing off that tail of his," he said to himself.

One cold winter day Brother Fox came by Rabbit's house with a big string of fish he had just caught. "MMMmmm!" said Brother Rabbit. "How I wish I had some of those fish! How did you catch them, Brother Fox?"

Now Brother Fox had caught the fish in the ordinary way—with a pole and a line and a hook. But he said to Rabbit, "Why, I just sat on the edge of the pond and let my tail dangle in the water! When enough fish had grabbed on to my tail, I pulled them out!"

Brother Rabbit went right down to the pond. He sat with his back to it and hung his long bushy tail in the cold, cold water. He sat there for hours, but he didn't feel even one fish grab his tail.

Pretty soon it got dark out and the cold winter wind began to blow.. "Brrr…!" said Rabbit. "It's too cold out here. Fish or no fish, I'm going home!"

But when Brother Rabbit tried to pull his tail out of the pond, he couldn't do it. The pond had frozen solid, and his tail was stuck in the ice. Rabbit began to cry and wail. "Help, help!" he hollered. "Somebody help me!"

Now Brother Owl just happened to be flying overhead, and he heard Rabbit yelling for help. He swooped down and saw the predicament Rabbit was in.

"Quit hollering!" said Owl. "I'll pull you right out of there." So Owl grabbed Brother Rabbit's left ear and began to pull and pull. That left ear began to get longer and longer, and Rabbit was *still* stuck in the ice.

"Ow! Ow!" cried Rabbit. "If we have to keep doing this, you better start pulling on my right ear so at least it will match the left one."

So Brother Owl began to pull on the right ear, and it got longer and longer, too. And finally, with a strong pull and a loud *Crack* and *Pop*, Brother Rabbit's tail snapped right off and he was free of the ice at last.

To this very day, Rabbit has long ears and a short tail. And he doesn't go fishing anymore, either!

WHY RABBIT HAS LONG EARS AND A SHORT TAIL

Rabbit Before, Rabbit After

Color and cut out all the parts. Get a piece of paper and draw a line down the middle. On the right-hand side, paste parts to show what Brother Rabbit looked like a long time ago. On the left-hand side, paste parts to show what he looks like now. Then write a sentence that describes each picture.

WHY CHICKENS AND HAWKS ARE ENEMIES
GHANAIAN

◆ **OBJECTIVE:** To predict what will happen in a "why" story

◆ **STORY SUMMARY:** A hawk works hard to make drums for a party, then asks his friend, a chicken, to refrain from playing them while he goes off to get food. The chicken promises, but then breaks his promise and plays the drums. The hawk hears the drum song, flies back, and gets into a fight with the chicken. While the two birds are fighting, humans come and take the drums and make them theirs forever.

SUGGESTED PROCEDURE

1. After reading the story title, discuss how real-life hawks get food by eating smaller birds, including domestic ones like chickens. Ask students to predict what this story will explain in a make-believe way and how the chicken and hawk will behave at the *beginning* of the story (as friends).

2. As you read the story aloud, pause after the phrase "…and the hawk still wasn't back." Invite students to predict what will happen next. Ask them to check their predictions as they listen to the rest of the story.

3. Invite students to tell what other "why" the story explains (why people have drums). Then invite students to fill in the data for this tale on the Story Stair Organizer.

4. Suggest that writing partners make captioned pictures that tell the story. After sharing these with the class, students can include their retellings in their portfolios.

FOLLOW-UP ACTIVITIES

1. Write the words of the recurring drum song on the chalkboard. Invite students to say the words chorally as you come to them in a retelling of the story.

2. Distribute copies of Activity Sheet 13 and help students make their puppets. Then provide small hand drums for partners to play as they enact a puppet story.

3. As a critical-thinking activity, ask students to compare this "why" story and the story "Why Rabbit Has Long Ears and a Short Tail" with the fables they read. How are the characters alike? (They are animals who talk as humans do.) What is the moral of the story? No moral is directly stated, but it may be inferred. The moral of "Why Chickens and Hawks Are Enemies" might be interpreted as: Broken promises lead to broken friendships.

Why Chickens and Hawks Are Ememies

A long time ago, the chicken and the hawk were good friends. In fact, they were such good friends that they decided to give a party.

The hawk said, "I'll make some talking drums for the party. I'll make them out of the trunks of trees. I'll put beautiful carvings on them. After the drums have dried in the sun, they will be fit for playing."

The hawk worked many days to make those drums. The chicken just sat around and watched him. When the hawk finished his work, he was very hungry. He said to the chicken, "While the drums are drying, I'm going to fly off and find myself some food. Now, don't you touch those drums, Chicken! I'm the one who worked to make them, so I'm the one who gets to play them first!"

The chicken promised. But as the hours went by, the urge to try the drums got stronger and stronger, and the hawk still wasn't back.

The chicken thought to himself, "What harm would it do to just play a little song on those drums? A very soft song." So the chicken tried it. Very softly he tapped out:

Da-dum, da-dum,
This is fun!

In fact, it was so much fun that the chicken tried it again and again, and each time the song got louder:

DA-DUM, DA-DUM
THIS IS FUN!
and *louder*!
DA-DUM, DA-DUM
THIS IS FUN!

Pretty soon the song was so loud that the hawk could hear it from a long way off. He was mad as could be, and went flying back to where the chicken sat playing the drums and singing.

"You broke your promise!" hollered the hawk to the chicken. They got into a terrible fight. Feathers flew and squawks sounded as the two birds tumbled and shrieked and bit each other.

While the birds were fighting, some people came along and found the drums and took them. "These are our drums now," said the people. Forever after that, the talking drums belonged to the people. They used the drums as they told stories and acted them out and sent messages to each other.

And forever after that, the hawk and the chicken have been enemies.

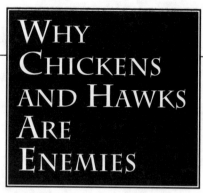

WHY CHICKENS AND HAWKS ARE ENEMIES

Puppet Players

Color the puppets. Then cut them out along the dotted lines. Paste the tabs at the end to make a loop that fits over your finger. Use your finger puppets to tell a story.

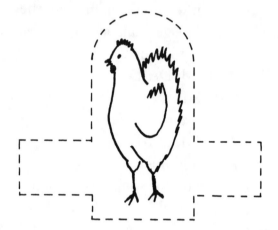

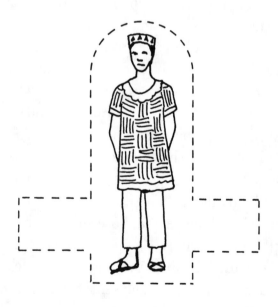

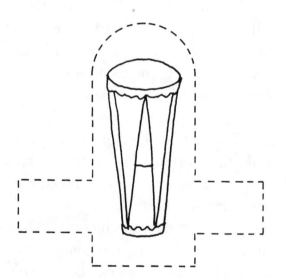

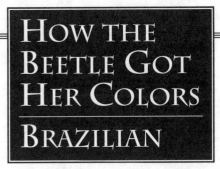
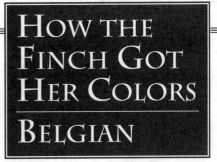

HOW THE BEETLE GOT HER COLORS
BRAZILIAN

HOW THE FINCH GOT HER COLORS
BELGIAN

◆ **OBJECTIVE:** To compare "why" stories from different cultures

◆ **STORY SUMMARY:** In the story from Brazil, a beetle wins glorious colors by flying to the finish line, much to the surprise of the other contestant, a boastful rat who was unaware that the humble beetle has wings. In the story from Belgium, an obedient and shy finch is left without colors after other birds push ahead of her in line to get colored feathers from the rainbow. The Great Bird rewards the finch for her patience by giving her a little of every color.

SUGGESTED PROCEDURE

1. Discuss the colors that people all over the world see as they look at animals; plants; and natural phenomena such as sunsets, rainbows, and ocean waves. Invite students to name their favorite colors, give examples of where they see them, and finally discuss what the world would be like if there were no colors. Invite students to listen to the two stories to find out make-believe explanations of how two animal heroines won colors.

2. Read the stories straight through. Ask students to listen for the ways in which the heroines are alike and different, both in their appearance and in their behavior. Discuss these similarities and differences when you finish reading the second story. What personal qualities are rewarded? How are the birds in the second story like the rat in the first one? Why do storytellers in different parts of the world think that *colors* are a wonderful thing to win?

3. Invite students to enter the data for this story on the Story Stair Organizer. Students can also illustrate the "steps" in the story.

4. Invite the class to retell their favorite of these stories as you transcribe it.

FOLLOW-UP ACTIVITIES

1. Distribute and discuss Activity Sheet 14. Provide nature encyclopedias and simple field guides in which student partners can look up the animals and then color them correctly. Game partners can take turns selecting cards from a face-down pile and making up stories about how the animals got their colors. Invite partners to tell their stories aloud to the class.

2. Invite groups of students to act out one of the stories.

How the Beetle Got Her Colors

A long time ago Beetle was just plain gray. Rat used to make fun of her. "You ugly little thing!" he teased. "Of all the animals in the forest, you are surely the plainest. You don't have a beautiful brown furry coat like me. You don't have a gold coat and black spots like the jaguar. You don't have feathers of gold and green and blue and red like Parrot over there. If I were as plain as you, I'd hide all day in the bushes!"

Now, Parrot sat high in a tree, and day after day he listened to Rat tease poor Beetle. Parrot didn't like what he heard. So one day he said, "I propose a race between Rat and Beetle. The prize will be a beautiful coat of any color the winner wishes."

"Ho, Ho!" squealed Rat. "This will be an easy race to win. I can run very fast on my four strong legs, while Beetle can only creep along on her six tiny, skinny ones."

The race began, and as Rat dashed ahead he thought about the coat he would claim when he won the race. "While I like my brown coat," he thought as he scurried along, "I think I will have parrot add a gold stripe down the back, or maybe a few beautiful green spots on top of my head. No, maybe I'll ask for *blue* stripes and *red* spots."

Whenever Rat looked behind him, Beetle was nowhere in sight. Rat felt sure of victory. "Silly little Beetle!" he thought. "What nerve she has to think she can win a race with me! How I'll laugh at her when I'm wearing my beautiful new coat!"

But when Rat reached the finish line, there was Beetle waiting for him! "How can this be?" cried Rat. "How did you win, you slow, plain little thing?"

"I flew," said Beetle.

"You *flew*?" said Rat angrily. "I didn't know you could *fly*!"

Parrot laughed from the treetop. "After this," he said to Rat, "don't judge others by their appearance. Even the plainest-looking creatures may have powers that you lack."

Rat went grumbling off through the forest. As for Beetle, she chose a coat as green as the trees and as gold as the sun. And those are the colors she has to this very day.

HOW THE FINCH GOT HER COLORS

A long time ago all the birds in the world were gray. They didn't have the wonderful colors they have today.

One day the Great Bird who ruled them all saw a rainbow in the sky and had an idea.

"Line up, birds," he called. "I'll give each one of you some of these splendid colors."

How excited the birds were! They began to push and shove to get to the head of the line.

"I want blue!" hollered the jay. "Give me blue!"

"Give me yellow," shouted the oriole.

The parrot squawked "Give me orange and green!"

"Out of the way!" whistled the cardinal. "I want red!"

And so it went, as the greedy birds bumped into one another and held out their wings for the colors they wanted.

Finally all the colors from the rainbow were used up, and the birds stood before the Great Bird in their splendid new feathers. Then the Great Bird spied Finch. She was still as gray and plain as she had always been.

"Why didn't you choose a color, Finch?" asked the Great Bird.

"Well, I *wanted* a color," said the finch sadly, "but I was waiting for my turn, and now all the colors are gone."

The Great Bird looked angrily at all the others. "You selfish, greedy things!" he said. "I have a good mind to take all your colors away so that you will all be gray again."

The birds looked at one another, feeling a little ashamed.

"But instead of taking *all* your colors away," the Great Bird went on, "I'll take just a little bit of each color and give them to the finch. Pass before me, please!"

So the birds lined up, quietly this time, and walked slowly by the Great Bird. He took a bit of blue, some yellow, some green, some red, some pink—some of *every* color, and gave them to the finch, and then he smoothed them together on her feathers.

And that is the way the finch is to this very day.

HOW THE BEETLE GOT HER COLORS

HOW THE FINCH GOT HER COLORS

Animal "How" Game

Color the animals with a partner. Cut out the cards. Shuffle them and put them in a stack face down. Take turns drawing the cards and making up stories that tell how each animal got its colors.

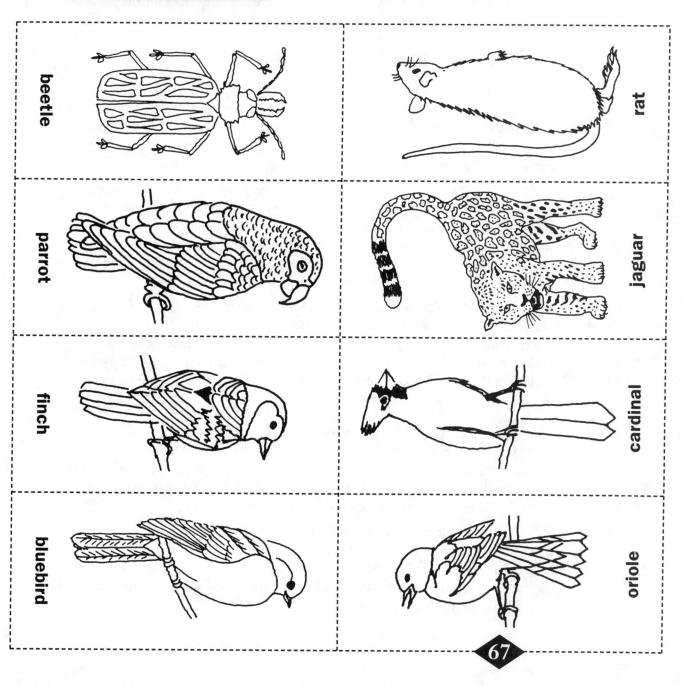

beetle

rat

parrot

jaguar

finch

cardinal

bluebird

oriole

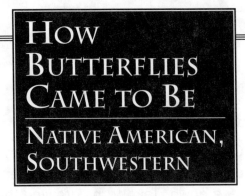

HOW BUTTERFLIES CAME TO BE

NATIVE AMERICAN, SOUTHWESTERN

◆ **OBJECTIVE:** To identify values stressed in legends

◆ **STORY SUMMARY:** In this tale from the Papago (a Southwestern U.S. tribe), Elder Brother recognizes the happiness that nature brings to human beings. He foresees the time when humans will suffer hardships, and—to help them through tribulations ahead—creates butterflies for them to see and remember nature's beauty.

SUGGESTED PROCEDURE

1. Display photographs or drawings of various butterflies and invite students to tell about the colors and movements of butterflies they have seen. Create a list of descriptive words and phrases that students suggest that tell how they feel when they see butterflies. Then ask them to listen to the story to hear how one group of people explains why butterflies were created.

2. After reading the story straight through, discuss Elder Brother's motives and concerns. (He made butterflies to add to the beauty of the world, because he was concerned about human happiness.) Help students determine whether human happiness is a real concern of real people in today's world and to give examples from their own lives or from news stories they have heard. Stress that some "why" stories tell about very important ideas; these stories are called *legends*.

3. To help students think critically, ask them to identify the fantasy elements in the story (the way Elder Brother made the butterflies; the dialogue between Elder Brother and the birds). Encourage students to tell how they know these episodes are make-believe. Conclude the discussion by asking students to review what is real and serious in the legend (Step 2, above). Have students enter the data for this story on the Story Stair Organizer.

FOLLOW-UP ACTIVITIES

1. After students complete Activity Sheet 15, ask them to work with a writing partner to retell the story from the butterflies' point of view. After sharing these stories with classmates, students can include them in their portfolios.

2. Provide students with grab bags filled with colorful scraps, paste, and tape. Invite students to use materials from the bags to construct new, beautiful animals or plants, and to name their creations. Students can share their inventions with classmates by pretending they are Elder Brother, pulling the invention from a bag, and telling why it will make people happy.

How Butterflies Came to Be

Long ago, when the world was very new, Elder Brother walked around Earth to enjoy the beauty of it. He watched the children playing. Everywhere on Earth, they were playing.

"How happy the children are!" thought Elder Brother. "They love the soft rain, the songs of birds, the colors of flowers, the green of the grass. They love the bright leaves that fall from the trees and fly through the breeze."

But as he watched, Elder Brother began to worry. "Someday these children may be sad," he thought. "They may get sick or be hungry. They may get cold in the snow, or be blown about by harsh winds."

Then Elder Brother had an idea that made him smile again. He got a big bag and filled it with flowers and red and yellow leaves. He put in some blue feathers of the jaybird, some blades of green grass, some golden corn. He added a bit of sunshine.

At the very last minute, he added some bird songs. Then he closed the bag and shook it and shook it.

"Now come here and open this bag," called Elder Brother to the children. The children did so, and out flew thousands of tiny, wonderful, colorful creatures with wings. They were of the colors of all the things in the world, and each creature sang a song.

"What are they? What are they?" cried the children. They laughed and clapped with joy as the creatures flew about their heads.

"These are new creatures called *butterflies*," said Elder Brother. "I made them for you. If times come when you are sad, the sight of butterflies may cheer you up. On stormy days when cold winds blow, the memory of butterflies will warm your heart."

But the birds were not so happy as the children were.

"Elder Brother," complained the birds, "at the very beginning of the world, colors were given to all living things. But songs were given only to us birds. We don't think it's fair for these new things, the butterflies, to have our songs!"

Elder Brother thought about that for a while. Then he said, "Birds, you are right. From now on, the songs belong just to you."

So that is how it is to this very day. The butterflies dance and fly and make children happy. But they are silent.

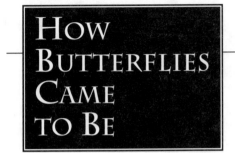

HOW BUTTERFLIES CAME TO BE

Your Butterflies

Color the butterflies. Then cut them out.
Put a string through the top of each butterfly.
Let your butterflies fly in your classroom.

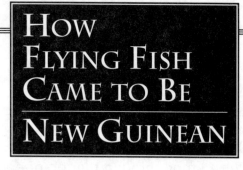
◆ **OBJECTIVE:** To recognize ecological concerns stressed in legends

◆ **STORY SUMMARY:** By accident, a man discovers a new kind of fish under a strange tree. When his neighbors arrive to enjoy a fish-feast, they lean on the tree, releasing the sea-water in it so that it pours out and becomes the ocean. As the little fish struggle to escape, the people gobble them up until hardly any are left. The man saves the remaining fish by commanding them to fly out to the sea where they can be safe and reproduce. However, he marks them with pink coral so that future generations can identify them when they go fishing.

SUGGESTED PROCEDURE

1. Discuss endangered species that students know about and why they are endangered. Explain that the old story they will hear now also tells about an endangered species. Ask students to listen to find out why the animal is endangered and how it is saved.

2. After reading the story straight through, discuss the "whys" that it explains (why there is an ocean; why some fish seem to fly; why these fish have pink spots) and the make-believe episodes of the story. Then discuss what makes the man in the story seem like one of today's environmentalists: He is concerned that a species will die out, and he finds a way to save it. Encourage students to compose morals or other brief lesson-sentences that apply both to the man's efforts in this story and to comparable efforts today.

3. After entering the "steps" of the story on the Story Stair Organizer, distribute Activity Sheet 16 and read the captions with students. Then invite pairs of students to draw the pictures and make their own mini-books.

FOLLOW-UP ACTIVITIES

1. As an evaluative thinking activity, suggest that students make a bar graph to show the relative seriousness or importance of the ideas in the "why" stories and legends they have read so far. Through discussion, comparison, and contrast, help students decide, for example, whether "getting long ears" is as important as "saving a species from extinction" or "providing the world with beauty."

2. As a prelude to "Writing a Why Story," invite students to brainstorm a list of what their own "why" stories might tell about.

How Flying Fish Came to Be

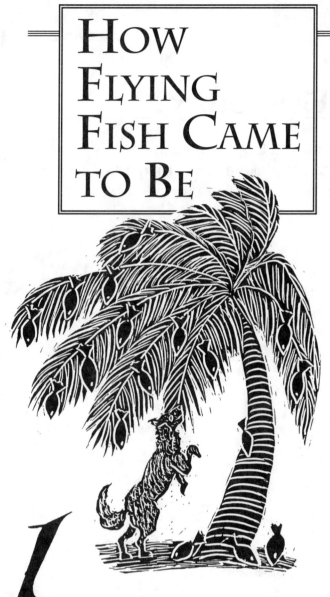

Long ago, there was no ocean. There was only dry earth, with a few lakes. Where was the ocean? It was trapped inside a huge sea-tree.

One day a man went out hunting. He took his dog with him. The dog ran up to a tree and began eating some small and sparkly things around the trunk.

The man was curious. He looked at the sparkly things. They were a new kind of fish. He tasted one, and it was good! "Look what I've found!" the man called to his neighbors. "New fish that come from this strange tree!"

Everyone in the village ran up to taste the fish. People leaned against the sea-tree and shook it as they gathered up the little fish. Suddenly the sea-tree burst, and all the water came pouring out and became the ocean.

At first the little fish did not go out into the ocean. They stayed behind and tried to hide in the mud. But no matter how they squirmed and looked for shelter in the oozy mud, the people found them and ate them. Soon there were very few fish left.

"Stop, stop!" cried the man to his neighbors. "Soon there will be no fish left at all!" But the people kept on eating.

So the man took the few fish that were left and threw them into the ocean. "Fly!" he said to the fish. "Fly away to the ocean to live and be safe." One by one, the fish did as they were told.

Then the man had another thought. In the ocean, these fish would multiply and there would be great numbers of them again. Then it would be safe to catch some for food. But how could the people recognize them when they went fishing in the great new ocean?

The man scooped up some tiny bits of pink coral from the shore. As the little fish went flying for safety to the sea, the man tossed the bits of coral at them. A bit of coral landed on the head of each fish.

To this very day, flying fish have a pink spot on their heads.

HOW FLYING FISH CAME TO BE

A Fishy Story

Draw a picture to go with each caption. Cut out the pages to make a book. Then make a cover for your book.

What grows on the sea-tree

What happens after the sea-tree is shaken

What the people eat

How the fish escape

THE FIVE WATER-SPIRITS

NATIVE AMERICAN, CANADIAN

◆ **OBJECTIVE:** To write a "why" story or legend

◆ **STORY SUMMARY:** This legend reflects an ancient, universal sense of some animating, human quality in inanimate things such as hills, wind, clouds, and water. In the story, five adventurous sisters go off for their usual day of exploring the countryside and climbing and sliding down rocks. On this particular day, the girls decide to climb the tallest rock of all and then slide down it. All afternoon and evening they slide down the rock. When the sun rises, the playful girls have been transformed into beautiful Niagara Falls.

SUGGESTED PROCEDURE

1. Read the legend straight through. If possible, show an encyclopedia picture of Niagara Falls and explain that this legend tells about the origin of the falls. Then discuss waterfalls students have seen and the colors and sounds they associate with them. Why do these phenomena make waterfalls seem almost alive? Discuss other inanimate things that—in our imaginations—we sometimes feel are like people, such as trees swaying and bending on a stormy night, or craggy mountains whose shapes, viewed from a distance, look like people or animals. Make a list of students' ideas.

2. Invite students to work with partners or in small groups to write their own "why" stories. Suggest that they refer to the lists generated in Step 1 above and in Follow-Up Activity 2 of the previous story to get ideas for their stories; or students can think of still other "whys." Have students enter the data for this story on the Story Stair Organizer.

3. Distribute copies of the Activity Sheet 17 for students to use as they develop their stories. Invite them to include the activity sheets in their portfolios.

FOLLOW-UP ACTIVITIES

1. Suggest that students write and illustrate their stories or make picture-panels that tell the stories. Ask students to put their work in their portfolios. Display the class folder in the reading center.

2. Encourage students to share their stories by telling them aloud to a group of classmates or by acting them out with their partners or groups. Tape-record the presentations, then make the tape available for students to listen to as they read or look at the same stories in the class folder.

3. Suggest that students complete their individual portfolios with a statement about the "why" story they liked best. Encourage them to give reasons for their choices.

THE FIVE WATER-SPIRITS

BY MARGARET BEMISTER

Once upon a time a grey, old man lived on the top of a mountain where he could see glimpses of the sea. He had a lodge made of birch bark that shone like silver in the sun.

He had five beautiful daughters, whose names where Su, Mi, Hu, Sa, and Er.

One day the youngest said, "My sisters, come and we will go and play near the broad, blue sea, where the waves beat against the rocks." So away they ran out of the lodge and down the mountains side. They were all dressed in robes of snow-white foam that fluttered far behind them as they ran. Their sandals were of frozen water-drops, and their wings of painted wind. On they scampered over valley and plain, until they came to a tall, bare rock as high as a mountain.

Then the youngest cried, "Sisters, here is a dreadful leap, but if we are afraid, and go back, our father will laugh at us." So, like birds, they all plunged with a merry skip down the side of the rock. Then "Ha-ha," they cried, "let us try again." So up to the top they climbed laughing with joy, and down once more they went, nor ever stopped, laughing like girls on holiday.

The day wore on 'til sunset, and still they laughed and played. The round moon came up, and by its silvery light they sprang from the tall, bare rock, and climbed joyously up its side again.

Next morning, when the sun arose, the rock was no longer bare. Over its stony side poured great sheets of foaming water, and in the foam still played the five sisters. They never reached the sea, and there they still play, giving to us the beautiful Niagara Falls. Sometimes, if you look closely, their forms may be seen in the white foam, but always in the sunny spray you may see their sandals and their wings.

Writing a "Why" Story

Fill in the chart below to plan your "why" story.
Then use it to write a story.

PLANS FOR MY "WHY" STORY

The title of my story:

The main character in my story:

At the beginning of the story, this is how things are:	At the end of the story, this is how things have changed:

Here are the main actions that make the change happen:

1.

2.

3.

FAIRY TALES

CHARACTERISTICS OF FAIRY TALES

Fairy tales are stories in which recognizably human characters become involved in a world of magic and enchantment. A fairy tale has many or all of the following elements:

◆ stock characters who are either all bad or all good;

◆ a magic being or object who is either helpful or threatening to the hero or heroine;

◆ a task that the hero or heroine must complete;

◆ a reward for the hero or heroine; and

◆ repetitive features, such as: predictable beginning and ending phrases ("Once upon a time…" and "They lived happily ever after."); and recurring duos or triumverates, such as "two sisters," "three wishes," or a task that must be done three times.

Along with the magic are comparatively realistic heroes and heroines. Often, they are young people who face problems such as poverty, ridicule, loss, or abandonment, but who triumph over these adversities through kindness, courage, intelligence, and fidelity.

WHOLE-CLASS SECTION PROJECT

To enhance students' enjoyment of the tales and to help them write fairy tales of their own, create a large oaktag Fairy Tales Chart Organizer. Invite children to fill in the relevant columns for each tale as you discuss it. The sample shows possible entries for the first tale, "The Three Feathers." Hang the chart in an accesible place for students to refer to as they read each story in this section.

Fairy Tale	Good People	Bad People	Magic	Tasks	Rewards	Special Beginning and Ending Words
The Three Feathers	Noodle King	Noodle's brothers	a toad that is really a princess	to bring the King a carpet, a ring, and a beautiful woman	Noodle inherits the Kingdom	Once upon a time. They lived happily ever after.
Rhodopis and Her Golden Sandals						

THE THREE FEATHERS

GERMAN

◆ **OBJECTIVE:** To recognize major characteristics of fairy tales

◆ **STORY SUMMARY:** An old king must decide which of his three sons is fit to inherit his crown. To test their abilities, he assigns three tasks to them, ordering each boy to follow one of three feathers the king blows into the air. The older boys are lazy and arrogant in going about the tasks. The youngest boy, faithful and serious, completes the tasks and wins the kingdom through the help of a magic toad.

SUGGESTED PROCEDURE

1. Read the story straight through. Distribute Activity Sheet 18 and explain that under each illustration students are to describe what is happening in that part of the story.

2. Suggest that students include the sheets in their portfolios.

3. Display the Fairy Tales Chart Organizer. As you discuss the story with the class, ask questions like the following to help students fill in the chart:

- Who are the good people in this story? Who are the bad people?
- What task are the brothers supposed to do?
- What magic beings and events are in the story?
- What is the reward? Who gets it? Why?
- What number turns up a lot in this story? (3)
- What words begin the story? What words end it?

4. Call on volunteers to tell about other fairy tales they know that have similar characteristics to the ones they've listed.

FOLLOW-UP ACTIVITIES

1. Invite a small group of students to choose roles and act out the story in pantomime as you read it again.

2. Cooperative-learning groups can plan and act out their own versions of the tale, perhaps changing the setting, the tasks, the hero and villains, or the magic being. You may wish to have students re-enact the tale with three daughters instead of three sons. Lead students in a discussion about whether it's appropriate to value people based on their beauty instead of their character.

3. Cooperative-learning groups can begin to plan and draw Fairy Tale Castles on large sheets of oak tag. As they read each story in this section they can add the characters to their castles.

THE THREE FEATHERS

Once upon a time there was an old king who had three sons. The youngest son was so quiet and shy that his brothers called him "Noodle."

One day the king said, "I must figure out which of you boys is good enough and smart enough to inherit my kingdom. As a test, I will blow three feathers into the air. Each of you must follow a feather where it leads and bring me back the finest carpet in the land. As the feathers lead, so shall you follow!"

The older brothers chased the feathers that flew east and west. Noodle was left with the feather that dropped right down at his feet.

"Silly ol' Noodle!" laughed the older brothers as they galloped away. "He will never find a beautiful carpet *that* way!"

A mysterious door opened in the ground right under Noodle's feet. Bravely, Noodle went down into the hole. There he met a huge toad with bulging eyes and bumpy warts.

"What do you want?" boomed the toad to Noodle.

"Please, Toad," said Noodle politely. "My father, the king, has sent me to fetch the most beautiful carpet in the world."

"And for your courtesy, you shall have it!" said the enormous toad. The toad gave Noodle a carpet made of gold threads and woven with glorious pictures made of gold and blue and red. And Noodle said "Thank you" and climbed out of the hole and went to the castle.

In the meantime, Noodle's brothers had said, "Any old carpet will do for our father, the king!" They pulled big rags from a clothesline and carried the dirty things home.

"Well!" said the king. "My youngest son has brought home the finest carpet, so he shall inherit my land."

"What a silly idea!" said the two older brothers. "Noodle isn't big enough or smart enough to rule a kingdom."

The old king sighed. "Perhaps you're right," he said. "I will give a second test. I will blow three feathers into the air. As the feathers lead, so shall you follow! This time, you must bring me back the most beautiful ring in all the land."

The older brothers went after the feathers that blew east and west. The third feather landed at Noodle's feet, and his brothers laughed at him as they went galloping off after their feathers.

The mysterious door opened again under Noodle, and he went down into the deep, dark hole. The huge toad boomed, "What do you want *this* time, little fellow?"

"Please, Toad," said Noodle, trembling in fright. "My father has asked me to bring him the most beautiful ring in all the land."

"And for your courtesy, you shall have it!" bellowed the toad. The toad gave Noodle a golden ring all covered with jewels and carved with pictures of leaves and flowers. And Noodle said "Thank you" and climbed out of the hole and went to the castle.

In the meantime, Noodle's brothers had said, "Any old ring will do for our father, the king!" They made rings out of rusty horseshoe nails and carried them home.

"Well," said the father. "This should settle it! My youngest son has brought me the most beautiful ring, and he shall be king."

"What a silly idea!" said the two older brothers. "It's only by chance that Noodle has found a wondrous carpet and a wondrous ring. Altogether, he's too stupid to rule a kingdom."

"Perhaps you're right," sighed the old king. "I will give a final test. As the feathers lead, so shall you follow! This time, you must bring back the most beautiful woman in all the world to be your wife."

The older brothers followed the feathers that flew east and west. "Any woman will do for a wife!" they said. And one brother chose a lazy woman, fat as a sausage, while the other brother chose a woman wearing rags and tatters.

But Noodle followed the feather that had landed at his feet, and went once again into the deep, dark hole. The toad was larger, wartier, and angrier than ever, and its voice was like thunder as it said, "I am growing impatient with these visits! What is it, you want now, my boy?"

"Please, Toad," said Noodle fearfully. "My father has asked me to find the most beautiful woman in all the world to be my wife."

"And for your courtesy, you shall find her," said the toad. And before Noodle's very eyes, the toad changed into a princess so beautiful that Noodle had to blink his eyes from the shining of her. "All these many years I have been enchanted by a witch," she said, "doomed to be a toad until I found a young man like you, who is both brave and courteous." She went with Noodle back to the castle, and there was no doubt anymore in the old king's mind about who should inherit his kingdom.

"That's it, boys!" he said to his three sons. The older sons had to be satisfied with nothing, for nothing was what they had done.

As for Noodle and the Toad-princess, they lived happily ever.

THE THREE FEATHERS

The Tale in Pictures

Write what is happening in each of the pictures.

1. _____

2. _____

3. _____

4. _____

5. _____

6. _____

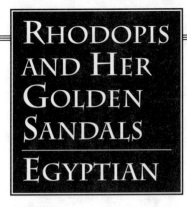

RHODOPIS AND HER GOLDEN SANDALS
EGYPTIAN

◆ **OBJECTIVE:** To find similarities in different fairy tales

◆ **STORY SUMMARY:** The Cinderella-type tale is the best known folktale in the world, with over 500 versions of it in Europe alone. Forms of the story appear on every continent, but its precise origin is lost in the mists of time. One Chinese version dates back to the ninth century A.D. The Egyptian version is even older, perhaps originating about 2000 B.C. In this tale, an eagle carries away the golden sandal of a poor girl, Rhodopis, who has been forbidden by her sister to attend the King's court. The eagle drops the sandal in the King's lap. He seeks throughout his kingdom for the sandal's owner. He finds Rhodopis, of course, and she becomes Queen.

SUGGESTED PROCEDURE

1. Ask students to listen to the story to discover what other familiar fairy tale it reminds them of. Then read the story straight through for students to enjoy.

2. Call on volunteers to tell how the columns in the Fairy Tale Chart Organizer could be filled in for this story.

3. Discuss other Cinderella tales your students are familiar with and encourage them to identify similarities and differences among them. You may wish to read or review one of the versions listed on the Bibliography (see page 108). Then suggest that students work with partners to complete Activity Sheet 19. Remind them to put the activity sheet and their copy of the story in their portfolios.

FOLLOW-UP ACTIVITIES

1. Invite student partners to choose similar characters from this and another Cinderella story, such as Perrault's version, and act out a conversation between them. Examples are: the magic eagle and the fairy godmother; the Egyptian King and the prince; Rhodopis and Cinderella; the selfish sisters.

2. Point out Egypt and the Nile River on a map. Invite interested students to look in encyclopedias to find pictures of clothing and buildings in ancient Egypt and show them to the class. Suggest that students who are making Fairy Tale Castles incorporate into their drawings some accurate details about this ancient world and its people.

3. Show some examples of ancient Egyptian paintings and discuss the "flat way" people are portrayed. Invite student partners to use that style to make a picture-panel story about Rhodopis. Suggest that students write a caption to tell what is happening in each panel. Display the picture stories on walls around the classroom.

RHODOPIS AND HER GOLDEN SANDALS

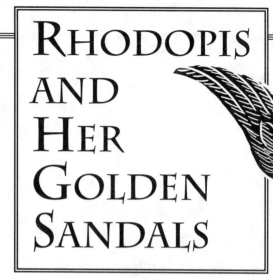

nce upon a time two sisters lived by the River Nile. Both sisters were beautiful, but only the younger one was kind, and her name was Rhodopis. She had only ragged cloths to wear. Her most precious possession was a pair of golden sandals, which her dear father had given her just before he died.

One day the older sister, all dressed in her finery, said, "Today I shall set out for the Temple of the King. He holds court there, watched by crowds of people. I'm sure that when he catches a glimpse of me, he will choose me for a bride."

Rhodopis said, "I want to go, too! I wish to see this King, for I hear he is a wise and just man who treats his subjects kindly."

But her sister laughed at her. "Stay home, you silly girl and tend the crops!" she ordered.

With a sigh and a tear, Rhodopis bade her sister goodbye. "Well," she thought, "before I go to work in the fields, I can at least take some time for a swim in the river." She took off her beautiful golden sandals, left them on the river bank, and dove into the cool waters of the Nile.

As Rhodopis swam, she day-dreamed. "How I wish I could pay my respects to the mighty King!" she thought wistfully. "Perhaps next time my sister will let me go with her."

All this while, a huge eagle circled above, watching Rhodopis. Suddenly the bird swooped down, grabbed up one golden sandal in his beak, and flew away with it. "Come back, come back!" Rhodopis hollered. But the bird soared away and disappeared over the horizon.

Now, in the Temple far away the young King was listening to the complaints and requests of his subjects. A poor man stepped forward. "Your Majesty," he said, "my fishing boat sank so I have no way of making a living. My house is falling down, and my wife and children are hungry. My babies are dressed in rags, and the youngest one is sick. But I have no

coins to buy medicine for her."

The King said to his Royal Treasurer, "Give this man some gold so that he can care for his family. No one in my kingdom should be so miserable!"

All the King's subjects were in awe of this act of kindness. Rhodopis's sister thought to herself, "If the King is this generous with a stranger, I can imagine the treasures he will give to me when he chooses me for a wife!"

But the King was thinking, "Miserable as that poor man is, he has treasures that I lack: a wife and children to care for, and who care for him. How I wish I had such treasures!"

At that very moment, the eagle flew above the temple and dropped the golden sandal at the King's feet. The King picked up the little shoe in wonderment. He knew in an instant that whomever this lovely sandal fit was meant to be his wife.

Standing and holding the sandal high for all to see, the King made his announcement: "What woman can fit her foot into this sandal? Whoever she is, I shall beg her to marry me."

Every woman in the Temple moved forward to try on the sandal. Rhodopis's sister shoved her way to the head of the line. But wiggle and push her foot as she might, there was no way she could get the sandal to fit. And so it went with all the eager women. Pouting and angry, Rhodopis's sister trudged home.

Though the King was discouraged, he was not about to give up. With his noble, he set out on a long journey throughout his vast kingdom, carrying the golden sandal on a golden pillow. Wherever he went, women came forward to try to make the sandal fit, but it never would. The King traveled hundreds of miles in his quest, but after a while it began to seem like a hopeless task.

Sadly, he decided to return to his Temple. On his way home, he stopped by chance at the farm where Rhodopis and her sister lived. There he asked for a drink of water. The sister ran forward to bring him a cup. As the King looked around, he saw a young woman far in the distance, working in the fields. She was singing a sweet, sad song, more beautiful than any the King had ever heard.

The King said to the sister, "Please ask that young singer to come closer. Perhaps she'll be willing to try the sandal."

Now, of course the sister knew by now that the sandal belonged to Rhodopis, for she had found the girl weeping over the lost shoe when she returned home. "Oh, that's just a servant girl," the selfish sister lied. "She's never worn sandals in her life!"

"I wish to meet her anyway," said the King. He called Rhodopis in from the field and held out the golden sandal to her. Overjoyed to see her precious sandal again, Rhodopis quickly slipped it on. She was happy to accept the King's marriage proposal, for she had always wanted a husband who was kind and just. They were married in the great Temple, and they lived happily every after.

Comparing Fairy Tales

Fill in the chart below to compare "Rhodopis and Her Golden Sandals" with another fairy tale you have read.

In "Rhodopis and Her Golden Sandals"	In Another Fairy Tale
The good person is:	The good person is:
The bad person is:	The bad person is:
The magic being is:	The magic being is:
The reward is:	The reward is:

◆ **OBJECTIVE:** To identify common themes in fairy tales

◆ **STORY SUMMARY:** The heroine is about to give a party and wants to invite a fearsome dragon who lives on a mountain top. Though her parents try to dissuade her, she climbs the mountain twice to proffer her invitation, and both times runs home in fear from the dragon. The third time, she summons her courage and approaches the dragon. Long an outcast, the dragon is so overwhelmed by Mei-Ling's kindness that he not only accepts the invitation, but turns his grateful tears into a river that becomes a source of water for the people in Mei-Ling's village.

SUGGESTED PROCEDURE

1. Read the story straight through for the students to enjoy.

2. After students have filled in the Fairy Table Chart Organizer with examples from this story, write the words *kind* and *brave* on the chalkboard. Invite students to tell how Mei-Ling is kind and brave, and then to tell about other fairy-tale heroes and heroines who exhibit one or both of these qualities. For example, in *The Three Feathers* the hero is brave enough to descend into a deep dark hole.

3. Suggest that students include the medallions from Activity Sheet 20 in their portfolios.

FOLLOW-UP ACTIVITIES

1. Cooperative-learning groups can add characters from *Mei-Ling and the Dragon* to their Fairy Tale Castles. Suggest that students use encyclopedias to find pictures of homes and clothing in long-ago China.

2. Reading partners can read the story of Mei-Ling together and illustrate it. Suggest that partners share their pictures with a small group of classmates and talk about the similarities and differences in the depictions.

3. Invite a Chinese student or a community-resource person to tell how the dragon is an important symbol in Chinese culture.

MEI-LING AND THE DRAGON

Once upon a time there lived a girl named Mei-Ling. Her family was poor, and indeed the whole village was poor! Rain seldom came to their land anymore, and the crops withered and drooped in the dry, dry fields. In addition to all this, the people lived in fear of an enormous dragon who lived at the top of the mountain. The dragon breathed smokey flames and bellowed in a terrifying voice. "Never go near the dragon!" the villagers warned their children. "He must be the cause of all our poverty and woes."

Now, when Mei-Ling's birthday drew near, her parents said to her, "Poor as we are, we want you to have a fine, big party. You may ask whomever you please."

Mei-Ling said, "I'll ask all my family and friends, and I will ask the dragon, too." And she started up the mountain.

"Come back, foolish girl!" hollered Mei-Ling's mother. "The dragon will eat you!"

Mei-Ling went halfway up the mountain. She could hear the dragon bellowing a fearsome song:

Alone I live, alone I roar.

I am a dragon evermore.

Fiery flames shot down the cliffs from the dragon's mouth, and Mei-Ling ran back down to her house. "I hope you've learned your lesson!" said her father.

The next day Mei-Ling's mother said, "Your birthday guest list is almost finished. Is there anyone else you want to add?"

"I want to add the dragon," said Mei-Ling, and she started up the mountain.

"Come back, silly girl!" hollered Mei-Ling's father. "The dragon will knock you over with his thumping, bumping tail!"

Mei-Ling went three-quarters of the way up the mountain. Now she could see the huge form of the dragon as he bellowed his song:

Alone I live, alone I cry.

Friendless and sad until I die.

Red-hot stones shot from the dragon's mouth and came roaring down the mountain toward Mei-Ling. She ran back home.

"I hope you've learned your lesson!" said her mother.

Now it was Mei-Ling's birthday morning, and all was ready for her party. "Poor as they are," said her mother, "your friends and family have prepared small gifts for you on this special day. A little rice from the barren fields, a few fruits from the dry trees. Is there anything else you would like for your birthday?"

"I want to ask the dragon to my party," said Mei-Ling. And she started up the mountain. Her parents called her back, her friends begged "Go no farther!" But on Mei-Ling went, until she reached the fiery top of the mountain. The rocks and trees shook with the dragon's song, and from his throat came dry, hot dust:

Alone I live. Who dares come near?

Who can conquer doubt and fear?

Mei-Ling said, "Though you are certainly a fearsome beast, I've come to invite you to my party."

The dragon suddenly stopped his roaring. "Never before in all my life has anyone dared to speak to me," he said. "You are indeed a child of courage, and of kindness, too! Climb upon my back, Mei-Ling, and we shall go back to your party together."

Mei-Ling did so, and as the dragon moved down the mountain, a cool and deep blue river suddenly appeared, and the dragon and Mei-Ling drifted on it to the village. Forever after that, the river provided water for the fields, so that the crops grew and the people were never hungry again. As for the dragon, he became a welcome visitor and a symbol of good luck. And as for Mei-Ling, she was honored by her people and lived among them happily ever after.

Fairy Tale Awards

Fill in the medallions with names of fairy tale characters that fit the descriptions. Color and cut them out. Then put ribbons through the holes so you can wear them.

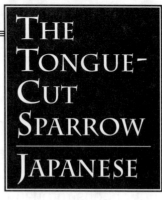

THE TONGUE-CUT SPARROW

JAPANESE

◆ **OBJECTIVE:** To predict what will happen in a fairy tale

◆ **STORY SUMMARY:** An old woman rescues a sparrow, who then thanks her by singing a song for her each morning. A neighbor is annoyed by the song and cuts the sparrow's tongue so that he can never sing again. The kind woman and her husband visit the sparrow to extend their sympathy, and at the end of their visit the sparrow wants to give them a gift and asks them to choose either a very small basket or a very large one. They take the former, and when they get home find that it is filled with gold and silk. The neighbor, making the same journey under the pretense of wanting to apologize to the sparrow, chooses the large basket. It is filled with nasty creatures who carry her away forever.

SUGGESTED PROCEDURE

1. Before reading the story aloud, invite students to refer to the Fairy Tale Chart Organizer and name the features they expect to find in "The Tongue-Cut Sparrow." Ask students to listen for these features.

2. As you read, pause at three or four significant intervals to ask students to predict what will happen next. Encourage them to explain their predictions on the basis of what they already know about fairy tales.

3. After students have filled in the Fairy Tale Organizer with examples from this story, distribute Activity Sheet 21 and discuss the directions. Suggest that students put their completed activity sheets in their portfolios after they have shared and compared their work.

FOLLOW-UP ACTIVITIES

1. As a critical-thinking activity, discuss how each fairy tale is different even though they all follow essentially the same pattern. What new details keep you interested even though you know everything will turn out "happily ever after"? As an example, invite students to compare and contrast the magical entities—the toad, the fish, the dragon, and the sparrow—in the fairy tales they have read so far in this section.

2. Invite groups of students to act out the story. Suggest that they incorporate the acts of courtesy (bowing to show respect, offering food to guests) that are important in Japanese culture.

THE TONGUE-CUT SPARROW

Once upon a time in a little old house in a small village there lived a poor woman and her husband. They had little to eat and very few possessions, but they took great pleasure in the trees and lakes and animals that were their neighbors.

One morning after a rainstorm, the old woman found a tiny sparrow on her doorstep. He seemed hungry and half-drowned, so the woman took him gently inside and fed him, then held him up in the sunlight so that his wings would dry and fluff.

When the sparrow felt better, he sang a happy song to thank the old woman. Then he flew away to his home in the forest. But every morning after that the sparrow came to the old couple's window and twittered his song again as the sun rose. The woman and her husband were thankful for this, for they liked to get up early and to be awakened in such a pleasant way.

But the woman who lived next door to the couple hated the sparrow's early-morning song. One day she caught him and slit his tongue so that he could never sing again.

When the kind woman found out what had happened to her friend the sparrow, she was extremely sad.

"Come," she said to her husband. "Let us try to find the sparrow's house so that we may offer him our sympathy."

The old couple trudged along the road, hoping to find someone who could direct them to the sparrow. "Do you know where the tongue-cut sparrow lives?" they asked a crow who was eating rice in the fields.

"I'm not sure exactly," said the crow. "But I think it's over that hill somewhere."

The woman and her husband slowly climbed the steep hill. At the top they met a field mouse who was gathering seeds in the grass.

"Do you know where the tongue-cut sparrow lives?" the woman asked.

"I'm not sure exactly," said the field mouse. "But I think you must go through the forest to find him."

The old woman and her husband were tired from their long climb, but they pushed on slowly through the deep woods, looking all about them for the sparrow's home. As they emerged from the forest, they met a bat who was sleepily hanging upside down from a tree limb.

"Do you know where the tongue-cut sparrow lives?" the woman asked.

"Why, yes," yawned the bat. "He lives just on the other side of that little bridge."

How happy the woman and the man were to find their friend. And the sparrow was equally delighted to see them. He bowed deeply as he welcomed them into his home, then introduced them to his wife and children, who hastened to bring them boiled rice and fish and watercress.

The sun was setting as they all finished their feast, and the old couple rose to go home, for they had a long way to travel.

"Wait a moment!" said the sparrow. He brought out two covered baskets, one very large and one quite small. "Please take one of these as a gift," he said to his visitors. "Choose whichever one you wish."

The old woman thought to herself that the large basket must have all the sparrow's treasure in it, and she did not wish to deprive him of this, so she chose the small basket, saying, "We have a long way to go and cannot carry a large, heavy basket."

The couple bowed deeply to the sparrow as they left his house. Then over the bridge they went and through the deep forest and down the steep mountain.

It was dark when they got back to their tiny house. The old couple, tired as they were, opened the little basket, thinking that it might hold rice cakes for their supper. Instead of rice cakes, though, they found piles of gold and rolls of silk, enough to make them rich for the rest of their lives. They were more grateful than ever to the sparrow.

Now, the mean old woman next door heard her neighbors laughing and talking. She crept up to their house and peered through the screen wall. When she saw the gold and the silk, she was determined to get some for herself. So the next morning she paid the old couple a visit.

"I am so sorry that I cut the tongue of your sparrow!" she said to the kind woman. "Please tell me the way to his house so that I can offer my apologies in person."

The kind woman told her the way, and off she went, dreaming of the treasure she would bring home. The sparrow was not happy to see her at his door, but his good manners prevailed. Bowing courteously, he invited her in and prepared a feast for her.

Just before she left, it happened as before: The sparrow brought out a large basket and a very small one, and asked her to take one as a gift.

The cross old woman thought to herself, "If the little basket held so much gold and silk, imagine how much the big one must hold!" She chose that big basket and struggled homeward with it. It was immensely heavy, and she had to pull and tug it over the bridge and through the thick forest and down the rocky hillside. When she got home, she eagerly opened the basket to see her treasures. Treasures indeed! Swarms of horrible creatures flew out of the basket and began to sting her and scratch her. Her cries were to no avail. The creatures finally picked her up and flew away with her, and nobody has seen her since.

But as for the kind old woman and her husband, they lived happily ever after.

THE TONGUE-CUT SPARROW

Fairy Tale Story Wheel

Fill in each part of the story wheel with a sentence that answers the question.

5. What is the reward for cruelty?

_____
_____
_____

1. What kind thing does she do?

_____
_____

4. What is the reward for kindness?

_____
_____
_____

2. What cruel thing does she do?

_____
_____

3. *How is he different, or magic?*

_____
_____
_____

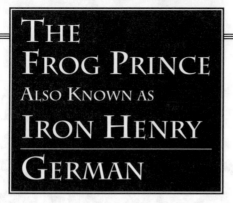

THE FROG PRINCE
ALSO KNOWN AS
IRON HENRY
GERMAN

◆ **OBJECTIVE:** To contrast and compare fairy-tale characters

◆ **STORY SUMMARY:** As the princess is tossing her favorite plaything, a golden ball, the ball falls into a deep well. A frog emerges from the well and says he will retrieve the ball if the princess promises to let him come to live with her in the castle. Although the princess is quick to make this promise, she doesn't want to keep it. Twice she turns the frog away. Twice her father, the king, tells her that "If you make a promise, you must keep it." He says this again when the frog demands to play in the princess's room. In a fit of anger, the princess throws the frog across the room, and it turns into a handsome prince, restored to his real identity because of the thrice-kept promise. As the happy couple rides away in a coach, the prince's coachman, Iron Henry, feels the iron bands of sadness break away from his heart.

SUGGESTED PROCEDURE

1. Read the story straight through for students to enjoy.

2. Discuss the character of the heroine in the story. Students will note that, unlike most other fairy-tale heroes and heroines, she is not kind or trustworthy, and only keeps her promises because her father tells her to. Have students brainstorm a list of words and phrases that describe her. Encourage the class to debate whether or not she deserves a reward.

3. Discuss the surprise character in the story—Iron Henry, who appears late in the tale. How is he different from the princess? Which character is a better friend to the prince? Why?

4. After students have filled in the Fairy Tale Chart Organizer with examples from this story, invite them to complete Activity Sheet 22 and play the game. Remind students to include their sheets in their portfolios.

FOLLOW-UP ACTIVITIES

1. Students can work in groups of four to make masks depicting the main characters in the story, then use their masks in an improvised play based on the story to present to the class.

2. Invite students to make Venn diagrams showing the similarities and differences between the heroine of *The Frog Prince* and the heroine or hero of another fairy tale.

3. As groups continue their Fairy Tale Castles, suggest that they prepare captions describing each character.

THE FROG PRINCE

ALSO KNOWN AS

IRON HENRY

Once upon a time there was a princess whose favorite plaything was a golden ball. One day, as she tossed her ball beside a well in the castle garden, the ball fell into the well and sank like a stone.

As the princess wept, a frog peeped out of the well and said, "Don't cry, lovely princess! I will get your ball back for you, if you make me a promise. You must promise to let me into the castle and then share your meal and play with me."

"I promise," sobbed the princess.

The little frog dove deep and brought the ball back. The princess grabbed it without even a thank-you. "Silly little frog!" she thought to herself. "Whoever would want a frog in their castle?"

That night, as the princess ate dinner with her father the King, there was a knock at the door. The princess opened the door, saw the frog, and quickly slammed the door in the little fellow's face.

"Now what was all *that* about?" asked the King.

"Just a silly frog that found my golden ball," said the princess. "I promised him that he could come to the castle."

"Well," said her father, "if you make a promise, you must keep it." He told his daughter to let the frog in, and the princess sighed and did so.

How happy the frog was! He hopped onto the dining table and began to eat from the princess's plate.

"Shoo, you wretched little thing!" said the princess, brushing the frog away.

"Now what was all *that* about?" asked the King.

The princess explained that she had also promised the frog to share her meal with him.

"If you make a promise, you must keep it!" said the King gruffly. "So share your supper with the frog!"

How disgusting it all seemed to the princess, as the frog sat at the edge of her plate and ate carrots and peas!

After supper the princess went upstairs to play with her toys. She heard a PLOP, PLOP, PLOP behind her, and when she looked around, there was the frog, following her.

"Scat, little warty thing!" she hollered.

"What was all *that* about?" called the King from the bottom of the stairs. The princess explained that she had also promised the frog that he could play with her.

"You must always keep your promises!" said the King. "Let the frog into your room."

The princess sighed and let the frog into her room. How happy the frog was to jump about among her wonderful toys! And how angry the princess was to have him there! "Nasty little brute!" she said, and she picked the frog up and threw him across the room.

The frog hit the wall with a THUD, and suddenly began to change. He became a prince, very handsome and strong indeed!

"I must thank you for all this," said the prince, as the princess sat on her toy chest, with her eyes popping out in wonder. "Long ago, a witch changed me into a frog. I could not become a prince again until I met a princess who kept her promises!"

The princess and the prince were married in the princess's castle. Then they got into a silver coach pulled by six white horses. The coach was driven by Henry, a sad-looking man who had been the prince's servant in the old days before the witch. And as the coach rolled along toward the prince's castle, there was a strange and loud snapping sound from the coachman's seat. It scared the prince and princess.

"Never fear," said Henry. "The sound is the snapping of the iron chains around my heart. For when my master was changed into a frog, I was so sad that I put these chains on my heart to keep it from breaking. Now that my master is restored to his original self, the chains are falling away, and I am happy once again."

So on the coach rolled, with the prince and princess and Iron Henry. And they all lived happily ever after.

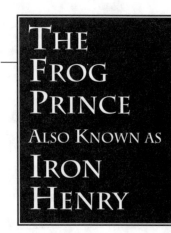

THE FROG PRINCE ALSO KNOWN AS IRON HENRY

Character Guessing Game

Choose six fairy tale characters. For each one, write descriptive words and phrases on a card below. Cut out the cards and write the characters' names on the backs. Show the descriptions to a partner. Ask your partner to guess who the character is, then turn over the card to see if he or she is right.

Description:

Description:

Description:

Description:

Description:

Description:

THE SINGING MONSTER
KENYAN

◆ **OBJECTIVE:** To write a fairy tale

◆ **STORY SUMMARY:** A rich widow who does not want her daughter to marry is beleaguered by a monster who destroys the crops in her fields. The monster glows in the dark and sings threats in a bellowing voice. The woman offers many riches as a reward to the man who can capture the monster. After two princes fail at the task, the woman raises the reward to include the hand of her daughter in marriage. A poor fellow who has loved the daughter from afar undertakes the task and captures the monster, which turns out to be a glow-worm, or firefly. The young people marry, and the glow-worm happily returns to its original home.

SUGGESTED PROCEDURE

1. Read the story straight through. Invite students to follow along with their own copies of the story and say the words of the monster's song chorally.

2. After students have filled in the Fairy Tale Chart Organizer with examples from this story, point out Kenya on a world map and review the common themes (in this case, courage) that appear in fairy tales everywhere. Invite students to compare the hero of the Kenyan tale with the heroine of "Mei-Ling and the Dragon" and with the hero of "The Three Feathers."

3. Discuss the completed chart. Then invite students to use what they know about the elements of fairy tales to write and illustrate a fairy tale of their own. Students can work independently, with a partner, or in small groups.

4. Suggest that students refer to the organizers as they brainstorm their original story. To make a story outline, students can fill in the story planning chart on Activity Sheet 23. Students can include the sheet in their portfolios.

FOLLOW-UP ACTIVITIES

1. After students have shown and read their fairy tales to the class, invite the audience to identify elements from the organizers that appear in the original stories.

2. Invite students to add to their Fairy Tale Castle. Cooperative-learning groups may wish to include characters from fairy tales written by group members.

3. After students have organized their individual portfolios, make copies of their original fairy tales and put them in the class Folktale Folder on a reading table.

THE SINGING MONSTER

Once upon a time there was a very rich woman whose husband had died. The only one left in the world whom she loved was her beautiful daughter. Though the daughter was old enough to marry, and wanted very much to do so, her mother would not let her. "I will never let my daughter marry," thought the woman to herself. "For if she marries she will leave me, and then I will be truly all alone!"

Now it happened one year that a strange beast began to come to the woman's field each night and destroy the young crops there. The beast glowed in the dark, and as it moved through the corn and millet and vegetables, it sang in a bellowing voice:

I cut the crops, I eat them.
I shake them, I beat them.

Each night the woman and her daughter watched and listened in dread as the glowing monster destroyed their food supply. Soon there would be nothing to harvest, nothing to eat! But the woman was too frightened to go near the monster, and she would not let her dearly-loved daughter even try. "For if she does," the mother thought, "the monster may kill her, and then I will be alone!"

Finally, when the crops were worn to a nubble and all the green sprouts ripped and brown, the rich woman said, "This must stop!" She gathered a pile of gold coins and purple cloth and said, "I will give all this as a reward to any young man who captures the beast!"

Now, this was pile of wealth to tempt many brave fellows. A strong and proud prince stepped forward and said he would capture the monster that very night. He set up a campfire at the edge of the field and waited there with his spear and his knife. But when the monster appeared far away on the edge of the field, the prince shivered and shook as he heard the beast's song:

I cut the crops, I eat them.
I shake them, I beat them.

As the glowing light came closer and the song grew louder, the prince grabbed his spear and his knife and ran back to the village.

The next day, the rich woman said, "Very well! I shall add more riches to the reward." To the pile of gold coins and purple cloth she added much more. Surely a brave young man would conquer the monster to get this reward!

Another fine prince stepped forward, armed with two spears, two knives and a huge shield. "With these weapons," he said, "no monster can defeat me." He sat by his campfire that night, waiting for the monster. But when it appeared, it seemed so bright and bellowed its song so loudly that this prince, too, ran away.

"Whatever shall we do?" cried the rich woman to her daughter the next day. Her daughter said, "Let's add to the reward. Let's promise that the young man who conquers the monster can have me as a wife." The mother's eyes filled with tears. "But then I would be all alone," she said. Nevertheless, she followed her daughter's advice and announced to the village, "Whoever kills the monster shall have not only all these gold coins and all this purple cloth, but also the hand of my daughter in marriage."

A raggedy youth stepped forward. He was the poorest young man in the village, and had not a sword or a knife or a shield to his name. All he had was the clothes on his back. But he was a good and intelligent boy who had loved the daughter from afar for many years.

"I will conquer the monster," he said. The villagers laughed at him. "With what?" they scoffed. They laughed at him as he set up his campfire at the edge of the field. "If princes cannot do the job, how can this poor fellow do it?" they said.

Night came, and so did the strange, glowing beast. The young man shivered as he heard its terrible song:

I cut the crops, I eat them.

I shake them, I beat them.

But his fear did not stop him. He approached the beast, while its light shimmered and pulsed and its voice bellowed. Tearing off his shirt, the boy threw it over the monster and wrapped the shirt tight, to make it like a bag. Then he peeked inside to see what he had caught.

There was a glow-worm!

"How glad I am that you've caught me!" said the tiny insect. "Scaring people is not my usual lot in life. But a witch, jealous of my lovely light, changed me into a monster. Only a brave fellow like you could break the spell."

The boy put the glow-worm in his pocket and returned to the village. "I have caught the monster!" he announced very proudly, as he pulled the glow-worm out of his pocket. Of course, no one believed him at first. So the boy touched the insect's tail, and the glow-worm began to sparkle and sing. Then everyone was quite ashamed to have been so afraid of such a tiny thing.

"Let's squash it," suggested one of the princes.

But instead, the boy set the glow-worm free in the forest, where it had always belonged and longed to be. The crops in the field were always safe after that. The rich woman's daughter and the boy had a wedding. They stayed in the village, in a house very close to the woman, so that she was not alone after all. And they all lived happily ever after.

Writing a Fairy Tale

Fill in the chart below to plan your fairy tale.
Then write it.

PLANS FOR MY FAIRY TALE
Good Characters:
Bad Characters:
Tasks:
Magic:
Reward:

BIBLIOGRAPHY

These recommended folk literature titles are excellent for reading aloud. Children can also read many of the books independently or with a reading partner.

The first section of the bibliography consists of single-story books. They are listed according to the general geographic region from which the original tale comes. Particular cultural or national origins are noted at the end of some listings. The last section of the bibliography lists collections of folk literature.

THE AMERICAS

Aardema, Verna. *The Riddle of the Drum: A Tale from Tizapan, Mexico*. Four Winds Press, 1979. (MEXICO)

Alexander, Ellen. *Llama and the Great Flood*. Crowell, 1989. (PERU)

Baker, Olaf. *Where the Buffaloes Begin*. Frederick Warne, 1981. (NATIVE AMERICAN)

Bang, Molly. *Wiley and the Hairy Man*. Macmillan, 1976/In Canada: Maxwell Macmillan. (AFRICAN AMERICAN)

Baylor, Byrd. *And It Is Still That Way*. Scribners, 1976. (NATIVE AMERICAN)

Belpre, Pura. *Ote*. Pantheon, 1969. (PUERTO RICO)

Blackmore, Vivien. *Why Corn Is Golden: Stories About Plants*. Little, Brown, 1984/In Canada: Fitzhenry & Whiteside. (MEXICO)

Bryan, Ashley. *The Dancing Granny*. Atheneum, 1977/In Canada: Maxwell Macmillan. (ANTILLES)

de Paola, Tomie. *The Legend of the Bluebonnet*. Putnam, 1983. (NATIVE AMERICAN)

de Paola, Tomie. *The Legend of the Indian Paintbush*. Putnam, 1987/In Canada: Bejo. (NATIVE AMERICAN)

Esbensen, Barbara. *Ladder to the Sky*. Little, Brown, 1989/In Canada: Fitzhenry & Whitside. (NATIVE AMERICAN)

Goble, Paul. *Iktomi and the Boulder: A Plains Indian Story*. Orchard, 1988/In Canada: Macmillan. (NATIVE AMERICAN)

Gobel, Paul. *Her Seven Brothers*. Bradbury, 1988/In Canada: Maxwell Macmillan. (NATIVE AMERICAN)

Haley, Gail. *Jack and the Bean Tree*. Crown, 1986. (APPALACHIA)

Hayes, Joe. *The Day It Rained Tortillas*. Mariposa, 1986. (NEW MEXICO)

Hooks, William. *Moss Gown*. Clarion, 1987/In Canada: Thomas Allen. (U.S. SOUTHEAST)

Roth, Susan. *Kanahena: A Cherokee Story*. St. Martin's, 1988/In Canada: McClelland & Stewart (NATIVE AMERICAN)

San Souci, Robert. *The Talking Eggs*. Dial, 1989. (AFRICAN AMERICAN)

Steptoe, John. *The Story of Jumping Mouse*. Lothrop, 1984/In Canada: Macmillan. (NATIVE AMERICAN)

Troughton, Joanna. *How the Birds Changed Their Feathers*. Bedrick Books, 1986. (SOUTH AMERICAN INDIAN)

Wolkstein, Diane. *The Banza*. Dial, 1981/In Canada: Penguin. (HAITI)

AFRICA

Aardema, Verna. *Bimwili and the Zimwi*. Dial, 1985/In Canada: McClelland & Stewart.

Aardema, Verna. *Bringing the Rain to Kapiti Plain*. Dial, 1981/In Canada: McClelland & Stewart.

Aardema, Verna. *Princess Gorilla and a New Kind of Water*. Dial, 1988/In Canada: McClelland & Stewart.

Aardema, Verna. *Rabbit Makes a Monkey Out of Lion*. Dial, 1989.

Aardema, Verna. *Why Mosquitoes Buzz in People's Ears*. Dial, 1975/In Canada: McClelland & Stewart.

Bernstein, Margery, and Kobrin, Janet. *The First Morning*. Scribners, 1976.

Bryan, Ashley. *Lion and the Ostrich Chicks*. Atheneum, 1986/In Canada: Maxwell Macmillan.

Climo, Shirley. *The Egyptian Cinderella*. Crowell, 1989.

Dayrell, Elphinstone. *Why the Sun and Moon Live in the Sky*. Houghton Mifflin, 1990/In Canada: Thomas Allen.

Dee, Ruby. *Two Ways to Count to Ten*. Henry Holt, 1988/In Canada: Fitzhenry & Whitside.

Grifalconi, Ann. *The Village of Round and Square Houses*. Little, Brown, 1986/In Canada: Fitzhenry & Whitside.

Haley, Gail. *A Story, A Story*. Atheneum, 1970.

Kimmel, Eric. *Anansi and the Moss-Covered Rock*. Holiday House, 1990/In Canada: Thomas Allen.

McDermott, Gerald. *Anansi the Spider*. Henry Holt, 1972/In Canada: Fitzhenry & Whitside.

Steptoe, John. *Mufaro's Beautiful Daughters*. Lothrop, 1987/In Canada: Macmillan.

Troughton, Joanna. *Tortoise's Dream*. Bedrick Books, 1986.

ASIA

Adams, E.B. Korean. *Cinderella*. Seoul International Publishing, 1983. (KOREA)

Aruego, Jose and Dewey, Ariane. *A Crocodile's Tale*. Scholastic, 1974. (PHILIPPINES)

Bang, Molly. *Tye May and the Magic Brush*. Greenwillow, 1981/In Canada: Macmillan. (CHINA)

Blia, Xiong. *Nine-in-One, Grr! Grr!*. Children's Book Press, 1989/In Canada: Weigl Educational Publishers Limited. (LAOS)

Brenner, Barbara. *Little One Inch*. Coward, 1977. (JAPAN)

Brown, Marcia. *Once a Mouse*. Scribners, 1961/In Canada: Maxwell Macmillan. (INDIA)

Cheng, Hou-Tien. *The Six Chinese Brothers*. Holt, 1979. (CHINA)

Duff, Maggie. *Rum Pum Pum*. Macmillan, 1978. (INDIA)

Galdone, Paul. *The Monkey and the Crocodile*. Clarion, 1979/In Canada: Thomas Allen. (INDIA)

Ginsburg, Mira. *The Chinese Mirror*. Harcourt, 1988. (KOREA)

Johnston, Tony. *The Badger and the Magic Fan*. Putnam, 1990/In Canada: Bejo. (JAPAN)

Lee, Jeanne. *The Toad Is the Uncle of Heaven*. Holt, 1985/In Canada: Fitzhenry & Whiteside. (VIETNAM)

Louie, Ai-Ling. *Yeh-Shen: A Cinderella Story from China*. Philomel, 1982/In Canada: Bejo. (CHINA)

Mahy, Margaret. *The Seven Chinese Brothers*. Scholastic, 1990. (CHINA)

Miller, Moira. *The Moon Dragon*. Dial, 1989. (CHINA)

Mosel, Arlene. *The Funny Little Woman*. Dutton, 1972/In Canada: Penguin Books. (JAPAN)

Mosel, Arlene. *Tikki Tikki Tembo*. Holt, 1968/In Canada: Fitzhenry & Whiteside. (CHINA)

Quigley, Lillian. *The Blind Men and the Elephant*. Scribner, 1959. (INDIA)

Towle, Faith. *The Magic Cooking Pot*. Houghton Mifflin, 1975/In Canada: Thomas Allen. (INDIA)

Troughton, Joanna. *Mouse-Deer's Market*. Bedrick, 1984. (BORNEO)

Yagawa, Sumiko. *The Crane Wife*. Morrow, 1981. (JAPAN)

Young, Ed. *Lon Po Po: a Red-Riding Hood Story from China*. Philomel, 1989/In Canada: Bejo. (CHINA)